BRIGID STONE

authorHOUSE®

AuthorHouse™
1663 Liberty Drive
Bloomington, IN 47403
www.authorhouse.com
Phone: 1-800-839-8640

First published by AuthorHouse 12/20/2010

ISBN: 978-1-4567-1928-9 (sc)
ISBN: 978-1-4567-1930-2 (dj)
ISBN: 978-1-4567-1929-6 (e)

Library of Congress Control Number: 2010918951

Printed in the United States of America

For my loving husband Mark,
for all his efforts and support during this endeavor
and for always believing in me.

Preface

Cork, Ireland 1982

THE BLOOD WAS POUNDING THROUGH her veins so fast it was all that she could hear, not the wind rustling the leaves on the trees overhead, not the cries of the night fowl as they flew overhead searching for their prey, not the squish of the soggy ground underfoot, nor her broken sob as she stumbled and fell.

Get up Margaret! You have to keep running! Yanking the hem of her torn, now dirty dress out of a thorn bush she dragged herself to her feet, her chest heaving hard, lungs torn by her ragged breathing, but she knew she would go on, she had to go on.

The full moon overhead filtered through the trees, the night air was cool. Even though the days still held the heat of summer, a thin layer of dew was already settling on the grass.

She had grown up playing in these woods, she knew every tree, every trail, but tonight she was making her own path, one she would never walk again.

Looking over her shoulder to where she had just come from, she couldn't see through the thick trees, but knew they were there, the row of houses where her family now slept.

Tomorrow was to be her wedding day, her simple white dress that she and her sister Ann had spent months sewing, late at night when the house was quiet, the days work put to rest, bent over the lamp light, giggling and sharing only the kind of sweet dreams young girls can before their loss of innocence, was laid out on the guest bed. Margaret Cahill knew she would never wear that dress, her innocence was gone.

I hope Ma and Da will forgive me… and Callum. Poor Callum, he will never understand and can never know the reason why I can't marry him.

She couldn't feel the tears running down her face until one dripped off the tip of her nose and landed on her pale white hand that she had placed protectively over her stomach. A small bump was showing, only noticeable to her, but she knew that soon she would be too big to hide the life of the unborn child that was growing inside of her. Stiffening her shoulders and sniffing her tears into submission she turned resolutely from her home and faced the darkness of the unknown in front of her, she started walking again.

Margaret had never known a man until a night six weeks ago, she had loved Callum and knew they would be married since the day he knocked her down in the school yard eighteen years ago, but they had never lain together.

Callum had been the insistent one, she recalled, even through the turbulent teenage years he had remained vehement that they deny their hormones and wait, wait for the day that they would be man and wife.

Margaret had thought the idea was quite foolish, after all if they loved each other, it shouldn't matter if they were married or not. She had argued this point with Callum many times, but he would just smile down at her, brush his work roughened hand over her cheek, and in his vexingly patient way say, "If we do love each other, it shouldn't be such a hardship to wait. I want you to be mine and only mine and I will have you, but only in the sanctity of marriage. It won't be so long, my heart."

How could a woman stand against someone so sweet? Someone who only wanted to do what was right by her and in the eyes of the Lord? So she had agreed to marry Callum, to be his wife and each other's first and only. But six weeks ago yesterday she'd been awoken by the sound of her bedroom window opening. She had thought Callum had finally grown tired of waiting and was set to welcome him with open arms, but when she had opened her eyes to look at him it wasn't Callum she saw.

Margaret stopped in front of a large oak tree; moss had grown up the base of the trunk from the ground where its large roots had pulled out from the soil.

This tree probably won't stand much longer, she thought as she bent her head back to look way up into its branches. Any good storm this winter and it won't be able to stand against the wind, too top heavy and not enough substance to hold it in place. *Maybe it was an omen.*

Trailing her hand along the rough bark she circled the tree until she found the place where Callum had carved their initials into the hardwood. She slowly traced the outline of the crude heart engraved around their initials and suddenly felt cold, a deep cold that seemed to radiate from the tree, through her arm and straight into her heart. Yanking her hand back from the bark Margaret shivered and drew her cloak more tightly around her shoulders.

All the warm memories this tree used to hold, of two young children stealing their first kiss under its canopy of leaves was now lost, she felt as if she would never be warm again, maybe *he* had done that?

He had literally taken her breath away. Turning from the tree, Margaret continued through the forest, feeling numb and thinking back to that fateful night.

Thinking Callum had changed his mind; she peered through the misty moonlight shining through her window, but the man she saw was not her sweet, innocent betrothed. No, this man was different. The moment his brilliant green eyes locked with hers she knew what was going to happen and she wasn't afraid, she wanted it, wanted him.

Margaret sat up in bed and tossed the covers off as she swung her legs over the side, her bare feet felt the cool wood floor in her tiny room, a gentle breeze fluttered the yellow curtains at her window, bringing the sweet scent of turf smoke into the room to mingle with the heady aroma of desire and lust, the air seemed to sizzle with it. Standing up from the bed, she never took her eyes off his. He was beautiful, the word seems too simple to describe him but there are no words that would be adequate. His face was all harsh angles, rising sharp cheek bones and a sloping, long, elegant nose, his complexion looked as if he were carved out of marble, pale, inexplicably smooth and hard, his eyes piercing green pinned her across the room, she could read the desire swimming in them and was excited as she closed the space between them.

She hadn't realized how tall he was until he was standing right in front of her, she tilted her head back so she could see his face, his lips twitched, was it a smile? A sneer? Who could be sure when all she could think about was having those lips on hers, tasting, probing, then suddenly she heard his voice, soft as velvet with violence around the fringe "Margaret, you are mine."

Had he spoken the words or had she only heard it in her head? The threat in those words sent a spear of heat down to her stomach where it balled, spread out through her limbs and made her shiver from the sensation. Being so focused on his enticing mouth she didn't notice when his hand raised between them, and with a few deft flicks of fingers he had the buttons on her front undone, the nightdress slipped off her shoulders and fell in a pool of cotton around her ankles, she stood naked except for the silver cross on a chain around her neck.

God knows she should have cringed when he touched her, everything about this man screamed danger, but God was nowhere near that night.

Forgetting Callum, forgetting she should be embarrassed in her undress, but she embraced it. She lifted her arms, which felt heavy with yearning, and clutched her fingers in his mass of black hair that fell to his shoulders as his mouth moved over her face, her neck, her breast, leaving searing prints of heat where ever he kissed.

Tearing his mouth from hers he snapped his head up, his eyes had gone dark and wild, his breathing fast and furious, "Now!" he growled as he shoved her down on the bed.

She should have fought, kicked, screamed, but she wanted him, needed him. She watched as he ripped his clothes off as if they were nothing but gossamer and tossed them in tatters to the floor, then she opened herself to him.

His hard body pressed her into the coarse mattress at her back, he was moving lightning fast now, his hands everywhere, touching, stroking, enticing, and stoking the heat inside her to a flame. He wasn't gentle, she knew he wouldn't be, his huge hands left marks, his teeth scraped her skin, but she reveled in every sensation, awareness alive in every fiber of her being. The moan ripped from her lips as he, throbbing, filled her. The sharp pain that comes with the loss of innocence was momentary; soon she was moving with him, matching his pace, meeting his passion, pulse for pulse, beat for beat. A thin layer of sweat glazed her skin as she came for the first time, she left marks in his shoulders the second, saw stars the third and fainted away into darkness as they came together for the last.

Everything was spinning, but the room was slowly starting to come back into focus. There were the shelves above her bed that held her favorite books, the scarred wooden bedside table, the heart-shaped music box sitting on it and standing there looking down at her was the man with the green eyes, the passion now cooled, he looked confused. Under his unfaltering stare Margaret suddenly felt self-conscious and sat up, bringing the sheet, she tried to cover herself. Pushing a mess of tangles over her shoulders with one hand while holding the sheet to her chest with the other she gathered the courage to meet his eyes, but she couldn't read the expression behind them and lowered her gaze again.

The silence was stretching into unbearable and finally she couldn't take it anymore, "What?" She had meant to sound strong and confident but it came out a quivering whisper.

"You didn't fight me." She shook her head, but couldn't bring herself to look at him again; he placed a firm finger under her chin and raised her head, "Why?"

"Because I fell in love with you the moment I saw you."

Hissing out a breath, he jerked his hand away from her face as if she'd stung him and turned his back on her. He stood silently staring out the window, the moonlight casting shadows over the contours of his naked body. She knew then he was going to leave her and her heart tore a little in her chest; she gasped at the unexpected pain and struggled to valiantly hold back the oncoming tears.

He never looked at her again, but said in a detached, lifeless tone, "You don't fall in love with Abaoth." And then he was gone.

She didn't rush to the window to look for him, she knew he was gone.

"Abaoth" his name signed through her lips, lips that could still feel his kiss. The passion fire he had brought her only moments ago had died and left her chilled and she began to shake.

She knew she loved him and he had to love her, why else would he have come to *her*? How could he have shown her all he had, opened her eyes to love and desire and not have felt it to? He would come for her again one day, he had to.

Covering her cold, aching body with the covers left on her rumpled bed, Margaret laid down and let the tears come, she cried herself to sleep that night, a broken-hearted woman, as her parents slept undisturbed down the hall.

BACK IN THE FOREST Margaret broke from her remembrance of that night, the night that had changed everything. She knew what he was, and if she was being honest with herself she had known from the minute their eyes had met, the man she loved and made love, wasn't a *man* at all. But that didn't matter, you can't choose who you love.

She had reached the end of the trail now and stopped, standing on the side of the county road that led in and out of her town. It was dark and quiet now, there would be no cars traveling to and fro until daybreak, when men and women would be traveling into Cork from the suburbs to work, at the Brewery or down at the harbor, or the women to go shopping. She knew her Father would be up in a few hours. Just before the sun broke through the sky he would walk down the stairs in their small two level house, he'd brew himself a pot of tea and sit down to the morning news with one of Ma's blueberry muffins before he headed off to work at the pharmaceutical plant in town; just as he has done every morning for the last twenty-seven years.

Thinking of her Father just back on the other side of those trees, she suddenly felt so alone, so lost. Oh not physically lost, she knew these roads and woods like a Murphy knows his stout, but emotionally she was in turmoil.

Looking down the dead road she began to doubt her decision to leave, she could see the city lights of Cork arching in the night sky just over the trees.

Maybe everything will be okay, she thought. It wouldn't be too difficult to pass the baby off as Callum's, a few months premature is all it would be. Feeling lightheaded and hopeful she turned back to the path leading into the forest, but looking back into the darkness under the trees, the woods no longer seemed familiar or comforting. Every shadow seemed foreign and sinister and she realized then that she could never go home again.

Margaret fingered the Celtic cross pendant around her neck and turned her back on the lights of Cork and the home she had once known and the people she had loved, and with only the clothes on her back, a fractured heart in her chest, and the child growing in her stomach, she walked away from it all and embarked on the unknown.

Chapter 1

Castleblayney, Ireland 1990

"I DON'T SEE WHY MAMA THINKS you're so special." a young girl at the tender age of seven whispered sulkily as she bent over the scarred wooden cradle that held her new baby sister.

She quickly looked behind her to make sure the door to the small bedroom was still closed, she didn't want Mama to overhear her saying such things, and breathed a sigh of relief to find they were still alone. Mama had changed the last few months before Alexia was born, she had always seemed happy with the way things were, just Mama and herself, "But then she got pregnant with you, and everything changed." she accused the baby as she turned back to look down on her small form with disgust.

She was swaddled in a pink blanket that used to be hers. In fact everything used to be hers, that cradle was the one she had used as a baby, now it was Alexia's, this room, even though it was hardly larger than the pantry closet in the kitchen, had been *her* room, now she had to share it with Alexia.

And Mama. Mama had been hers too, only hers, but now she was Alexia's Mama too. "Urgh! It just isn't fair!" she cried unhappily, forgetting to keep her voice down. Clutching her hands sheepishly over her mouth she peeked over at the bedroom door again, it was still closed. She didn't want to disturb Mama, she didn't seem to be her usual self these past few days; she just sits in the rocker, gazing out the parlor window, barely eats, and only stirs when the baby cries.

She didn't bother trying to get her mother's attention anymore, she'd stopped asking her to read a story or play a game, it wasn't worth having those sad, lifeless eyes look at her, but not see her.

Maybe she is still waiting for Da, she thought. Ever since she could remember Mama had told her stories of a father she had never met and after seven years of waiting, she had come to terms with the fact that she probably never would.

But he had come back, just as Mama had always said he would, for one night. But he hadn't stayed long enough to see her, the only proof she had of his visit is what's lying in the cradle.

It was hard to ignore the pang of rejection she felt prick her heart, but she pushed it aside; she had more important things to worry about. Turning her attention back to the baby, she knelt down on the wooden floor, pushed her scraggly brown hair that always had the habit of falling into her face, over her shoulder and leaned over the cradle.

Tilting her head to one side and crinkling up her nose, the pose she generally adopted when she was trying to figure out a difficult problem, she watched the baby stir.

She was waking from a nap, turning her head from side to side and emitting tiny squeaking noises, sounding a little like the mice that sometimes lurked around their kitchen.

"I suppose you're hungry now, huh?" she whispered as Alexia blinked open her eyes. She almost cringed at the thought of having to roust her mother into action to get the baby a bottle; she'd lost interest in nursing her within weeks of giving birth. "I suppose I could get it for you," she admitted reluctantly, there really was no use in bothering Mama when all she had to do was warm the ready-made bottle in a pot of water on the stove, "Shouldn't be too hard, I guess."

She looked down at the baby and met the big, sea blue eyes that were watching her closely. She'd managed to wriggle a small fist out from under the blanket and was waving it in the air and chirping in little high pitched bursts.

The sounds made her smile, "What are you trying to be? A bird?" she laughed and grabbed the flailing fist. The tiny little fingers clutched her middle finger and held on tight. "They're so small." she murmured as she rubbed her thumb gently over the little fingers holding her own, she couldn't help but smile, "I guess you are kinda cute." She hated to admit it but couldn't deny the fact when watching Alexia's chubby face break into a big gummy grin. "Just wait a minute and I'll go grab your dinner, okay?" She lightly tugged her finger free from the baby's surprisingly strong grasp and went as quietly as she could, down the hall and into the kitchen.

Dragging a chair from the small dining set that took up most of the space in the small kitchen she propped it against the counter. The Table and chairs had been second hand, the family who'd owned the house before them had left it behind, and no wonder as it looked like it had seen better days, but the child didn't notice things like that. She didn't see the gouges in the tabletop that bowed in the middle or the wobbly legs or half the missing spindles on the chairs, she only saw the many times her Mother had sat with her there, having tea and cinnamon scones, her favorite, or how she'd knelt on a phonebook so she could colour in her books when she'd been younger or the hundreds of games of snakes and ladders that had been won and lost while sitting in those very seat's.

She climbed on top of the chair, teetered above the stove to unhook a saucepan from off the iron hooks that had been screwed into the bottom side of the cupboard. Carefully she stepped down again and filled the pot with water placing it on the smallest element with the bottle of milk standing straight in it. After again using the chair to turn the burner dial to high she replaced it under the table and glanced around the doorframe into the sitting room where her Mama still sat, rocking slowly and looking out the front window.

Standing in front of the stove she waited as patiently as a seven year old can, shifting her weight from one foot to the other until the water finally started to bubble. Being careful not to burn her hand on the hot steam she quickly plucked the bottle out of the pot and headed back down the hall to the bedroom.

"Alright Alexia, here it is. I think it's the right temperature." She shook the bottle upside down until a few drops of warm milk fell on her wrist, just like she'd seen her Mother do.

She nudged open the bedroom door which was standing slightly ajar, when she noticed a pale blue haze of light just off to the edges of her vision. Her head snapped up, she quickly surveyed the room. The window was open; it hadn't been when she'd left. The warm summer air lingered as the day was fading into dusk, the sounds of Mr. Heaney mowing his lawn next door drifted into the room.

3

She closed her eyes to block out the ordinary vision of the room and opened up to her other sight. Focusing she could still see the blue haze, she knew it was moving fast, it was almost out of town, she would never be able to catch it. She knew what that blue haze of colour was, she'd seen it and many others like it before, different colours, different beings, but this one was a faerie.

The bottle thudded densely on the floor as she opened her eyes again and rushed over to the cradle, "Oh please, please, no!" She pleaded aloud as she dropped to her knees next to it, but it was no use, she knew what she would find.

The pink blanket that had swaddled Alexia was now loose and draped over the cradle, she could see it rippling and bunching from jerky movements underneath. With shaking hands she grabbed the corners of the soft material and lifted it away, an ear piercing screech ruptured from the thing beneath it, scaring her so that she dropped the blanket and jumped to her feet.

Alexia was gone. She knew it even before she had seen for herself, and in her place, thrashing and twisting around in the cradle, causing it to rock violently from side to side, was a faerie changeling.

"Oh no, oh no, oh no." she repeated over and over again as she looked at the creature.

Creature is the only word to describe it. It was as small as a human baby, but thinner, with long boney limbs, and hands and feet that looked like claws. Its skin was a jaundiced yellow hue, greasy tufts of hair sprouted every which way over its bulbous head, it was clothed in what looked like a swatch of sackcloth.

It's impossible to grow up in Ireland without knowing the lore of faeries and their changelings. As legend goes, every once in a while a faerie child will be born so hideous and so ill-tempered that the fair folk can't bear to even look at it. So they would take their unwanted child and switch it in the place of a human child, blonde, blue-eyed babies appeal to their sense of vanity, and that was Alexia to a tee.

Of course most people thought the old tales and folklore were just good stories and used them to scare children into behaving, but she knew otherwise.

The changeling was yowling its pitiful cries at the top of its lungs, its sunken black eyes were whirling about wildly in it's sockets as its arms bunched and its legs kicked, he looked terrified and she didn't know what to do.

Suddenly she spun around at the noise behind her, the bedroom door flung open and banged against the wall. There her mother stood in the doorway, her eyes confused. "What is going on in..." her question was cut off by a strangled gasp as her eyes were drawn to the tossing cradle. She slowly moved closer until she stood directly over it, "Mothers beware and watch your infant with great care, the faeries will take whatever they dare... No." the old saying whispered out of her mouth as she realized what had happened.

"You!" her mother screamed the word as she wheeled around, "It was you! You brought it here!"

She watched the emotion flicker over her mother's face, pain, fear, sorrow then anger.

The slap was so fast and so hard it sent her sprawling across the floor. In shock she held a hand to her stinging cheek, "Mama, it wasn't me, I don't know why they took Alexia." her voice quivered to a sob as the tears burned her eyes and down her flaming cheeks.

Her mother advanced on her, rage and anguish contorted her face until she was almost unrecognizable, "It was you, they always find you!" her shrill voice sliced through her head, along with the changelings high pitched whines as it became more agitated.

She backed away but her Mother snatched her by the shoulders and shook her, the force had her head seesawing back and forth until her teeth clacked together. "I'm sorry Mama, I'm sorry." her cries broke through the haze of fury in her mother's eyes.

"I'm sorry too, sorry you were ever born." With that she dropped her daughter into a tearful heap on the floor and left the room, her own sobbing followed her down the hall.

Her little heart was broken; her Mama didn't love her anymore. The tears wracked her body until she felt sickness roil around in her stomach.

Maybe Mama was right, she thought. They always do seem to find me.

Any creature or being that should only live in fairytale books are out there, living amongst us in the world, and they seemed to be drawn to her.

Wiping her runny nose on her shirtsleeve, she uncurled herself from a ball on the floor and crawled over to the cradle where the changeling was whimpering; her mother's wails of grief rang throughout the house.

Maybe Mama would love me again if I could get Alexia back. She wondered. If it was my fault and the faeries took her because they are attracted to me or something, then maybe I can find them.

She leapt up off the floor and ran to the bureau next to her bed; she pulled out a thin yellow sweater and pulled it on over her head. Then she yanked the summer sheet off her bed and looped it around her shoulder and tied it in a knot at her hip like a sash, then walked back over to the cradle. She tentatively picked it up from under the arms and held it in front of her while it kicked and tossed its head.

"Look, I'm going to try to take you back to your Mama, but I need to get you into this here sling, I can't carry you the whole way if you keep thrashing about." The baby stopped moving and looked at her almost as if it understood what she was saying. "That's better." As carefully as she could she tucked it into the folds of the sheet and swung it gently around so it was cradled across her back.

"I've seen pictures of Indians, they carry their babies on their back's like this." She shifted her shoulders, testing the weight and position of the baby on her back, it was squirming slightly but at least it wasn't screaming.

Not wanting to see her Mother, she opted to leave through the bedroom window; she slipped on her worn and raggedy runners and nimbly climbed through the window and landed on the soft grass below. Looking from side to side she checked to make sure no one had seen her exit and then made a dash for the neighboring yard where she could take cover in the smattering of trees until she reached the main road out of town.

The changeling protested to the jostling on her back, so she slowed to a stunted jog, she figured it best if no one saw or heard them and tried to move as fast as she could without upsetting *it*.

DARKNESS HAD FALLEN AND the changeling had finally fallen asleep in the sling on her back, she had been walking for three hours and was tired and hungry, her legs were dragging, her cheek still smarted from her mother's hand; she needed to stop.

She headed southeast, trying to steer clear of major roads and densely housed areas; she kept to the woods as much as possible. She didn't know where she was going but this was the way she saw the faerie's blue haze, for lack of a better word, heading.

Seeing a fallen tree up ahead she almost whimpered in relief and lowered her tired little body to sit on it. She gazed at her surroundings, she was in relatively thick woods, she couldn't see any lights through the trees but could hear cars traveling on the N2 not too far in the distance. She figured Carrickmacross was about four kilometers to the West of her; she'd made good time considering she was carrying a twenty-pound changeling on her back. Then almost as if it could read her thoughts the changeling awoke with an uproar, its ear-splitting cry cut through the stillness of the night like a foghorn in a church. She bolted off the log and would have started to run but she felt its pointy feet digging into her back as it struggled to be free.

"Holy Mother! You scared the life outta me." she scolded as she placed a hand over her racing heart and took a deep calming breath, "Ouch! Okay, okay, just a minute." It grabbed her hair and scratched her neck as it tried to fight free of the sling.

She untied the knot in the sheet that was around her waist and gently lowered it to the ground; when she bent over to try to untangle it from the blanket, she caught an errant tiny fist on her nose and leapt back.

"Fine, you just get yourself out of there." Crossing her arms in bad temper she sat back down on the log.

The changeling squirmed and wriggled its scrawny limbs until it wrestled free of the sheet and managed to sit itself up on the grass while it chirped in triumph at having gotten itself loose.

"You're a funny wee thing aren't you?" she eyed it skeptically, not sure whether to be amused or apprehensive. It snorted and gurgled in response.

They just sat in silence, watching each other through the darkness, until she felt her stomach rumble.

"Hmm, I guess I didn't think very far ahead. You're probably hungry too huh?" the changeling tilted his head as if trying to understand her meaning then scooted itself toward her on its bottom using its hands and feet to move along, its black eyes watched her almost hopefully.

She looked around again at the trees, tall oaks towered up into the star-speckled sky, "No fruit trees around here," she looked back at the expectant little face and sighed, "should have thought to bring some milk for you… hey, you just stay here." She held her finger up as if she were telling a dog to 'stay' then walked a little ways off to a bush she spotted. She started picking the marble sized green berries off of the branches and put them in the shirt she held out in front her. Having picked off as many berries as she could find on the sparse bush she turned and nearly stumbled over the changeling who was perched at her feet.

"Sheesh, you can be pretty quiet when you want to be. You scooted yourself all the way over here? " It just stared up at her with its mouth hanging open. Rolling her eyes she lowered herself to the ground and sat cross-legged in front of it.

"Here, they're gooseberries, not very ripe but I 'spect all the birds got the good ones." She held out a berry and quicker than a flash it darted forward and bit the berry from her fingers. "Hey take it easy, would ya! You got teeth, that's for sure." she regarded it dubiously as she sucked her sore finger, "Haven't you ever heard the expression don't bite the hand that feeds you? Well that applies here." She dumped the berries from her shirt onto the ground between them and watched it dive in grabbing handfuls and gobbling them up.

"Hey, slow down, you're gonna choke or something, and I don't know that thingy you have to do, the Heineken something or other." She laughed out loud as it lifted its face, berry juice dripping down its chin and smiled at her. At least what she thought was a smile. "Oh go ahead and eat." She waved it on with her hand and resignedly picked up a firm, green berry and bit into it. The tart juice squirted around her mouth and she spat it out, "Yuck! How can you eat those?" She wiped the back of her hand across her mouth and waited while the changeling finished up the last of the fruit and sat back on its bottom.

"Better now that your tummy's full?" It sighed, contented, and crawled up onto her lap, nestled itself in the crook of her arm and closed its eyes. "Tired are we?" carrying the little yellow skinned baby back over to the fallen tree she sat on the ground, leaned back against the log and grabbing the sheet that was still on the ground she tucked it around the changeling.

"You're really not so bad are you?" she whispered softly as she stroked its matted hair, "I don't even know if you're a boy or a girl faerie." It was already fast asleep, looking sheepishly around her even though no one was near, she gently lifted the leg of its tattered jumper and peeked in. "Boy. Well, sleep tight little fella." She snuggled down, trying to get as comfortable as possible against the hard tree and drifted off to sleep.

She woke just as the sun was emerging over the treetops; the sky shone a bright, burnt, dandelion gold, and the morning air was crisp and fresh with the scent of dew hovering above the ground where a fine blanket of moisture lay.

She felt the warmth of the changeling baby still cuddled on her lap before she even opened her eyes; every muscle was sore and she just wanted to stay asleep where there was no pain. She felt a tickle on her cheek and rubbed it away with her hand. She groaned when she felt another tickle brush against her face and opened her eyes to see a swarm of iridescent flecks floating around them, she clutched the baby closer to her body and blinked the sleep out of her eyes.

When she focused on the shimmering motes rippling and rising through the air she thought at first they were pollen, but they sparkled brighter then a flickering candle flame and seemed to be moving of their own accord.

She watched them, mesmerized by their tranquil floating when she suddenly realized what they were.

"You're Will-O-The-Wisps aren't you?" the sparks moved in unison, like a dappled wave of water as they flowed up and down, almost as if they were nodding in agreement.

She carefully rose to her feet, keeping the changeling tucked safely in her arms, "Are you here to help us?" the beams ebbed and flowed before her. "I know you're faerie lights and that you help searchers find someone who is lost." They started to spin in a great circle around her, creating a funnel like a tornado made of sunlight, the wind caught her hair in the updraft and flung the dirty and tangled strands wildly around her face.

"I'm looking for my baby sister; she was taken by a faerie and left this changeling in her place." she raised her voice almost to a shout to be heard above the roaring gale, "Please, help me find the faerie that took Alexia!"

The spinning stopped, she stumbled back a step from the abrupt change, catching herself she tossed the hair away from her face and beheld the wall of lights suspended before her as if they hung from strings. The baby stirred in her arms and she gently rocked from side to side to lull him back to sleep. Lifting her eyes back to the silent faerie lights, she whispered softly, "Please."

The lights started to drift one at a time like grains of sand being blown across a desert; they wove in a line into the trees on her left. She turned and followed them through the early morning light.

Chapter 2

SHE WALKED BEHIND THE SHIMMERING chain of lights for what seemed like hours. The trail of light lead her through the trees, on a course that was no easy to follow; considering the faerie lights were floating they weren't too concerned with navigating the best walking path.

Travel was slow as she ducked under branches and tripped over the uneven rocky terrain. Her pant legs were torn from being snagged on thorns, sticky briars clung to her socks and shoes. Her arms and face were bleeding from multiple itchy, red scratches caused from shoving through thistles and tiny twigs. She hunched her shoulders over the baby in her arms as best she could to save him from getting hurt, and by some miracle he remained asleep while she fought her way through the forest.

Tears of frustration and sheer exhaustion threatened to spill out of the corner of her eyes. She hissed as her head was yanked backwards, a knot in her hair had caught on a branch. Gritting her teeth she tugged and yelped when she broke free. Looking back she saw a clump of her brown hair hanging on the tree. She stamped her foot hard on the ground in anger and felt a shock of pain radiate up through her throbbing leg, "This is stupid!" Sighing, she shifted the changeling to her other arm; he kept getting heavier and heavier, she knew she wouldn't be able to drag her body much farther. Looking around she realized she'd lost sight of the lights.

"Where did those blasted things go now?"

Spying some flickers of movement through the thick brush to her left she battled her way to a clearing on the other side, panting and weeping she dropped to her knees and closed her eyes to catch her breath.

When she felt she could open her eyes again without falling flat on her face from fatigue, she looked up and noticed the faerie lights were stopped a few yards ahead. Were they waiting for her? She wondered.

"I can't do it. I just can't go any farther," she moaned. When they didn't move, just fluttered where they were, she peered through their collective incandescence and noticed they were hovering in front of something, something big.

Rising to her feet once again she limped over to them then through them. She was standing in front of a huge stone slab; it rose straight up out of the ground and towered up into the sky. Tilting her head back as far as it would go she squinted into the bright afternoon sun to see the top of it.

"What is this?" she asked as she turned her head to look behind her at the faerie lights, but they were gone, "well that's just great." she spat out incensed, "what am I supposed to do with a huge rock?" Looking to her left and right she spotted two similar rocks spearing up out of the ground.

Taking a step back she surveyed the whole clearing, there were more rocks, just like these ones, all arranged in a perfect circle, standing straight and tall like intimidating, rectangular soldiers.

"Eleven." she counted, "I've seen something like this before." her voice carried across the opening to the other side and seemed to bounce back from the encompassing trees.

"It's a stone dance. Like that famous one in England, Stonehenge." She ran her free hand over the rock in front of her; its surface was surprisingly warm and seemed to thrum with energy within.

"It's so weird, I've never heard of one of these being around here." She gazed down at the sleeping changeling in her arms; he'd snuggled closer to her body, with his little scrunched up face turned into her tummy. Somewhere along the way they'd lost the sheet he'd been wrapped in, she figured he must be cold and tightened her grip on him.

"This might be home for you little buddy, seems like a place a faerie would hang out."

Filling her lungs with a deep breath of fresh air, she mustered up all her courage and stepped between the stones and into the circle. The moment she broke the boundary the changeling jerked awake, his dark eyes as big as saucers as they wheeled around then focused on hers. He let out an agitated cry and his little boney body began to shake.

She shushed and reassured him that everything would be all right; she smiled at him and hoped he couldn't sense her own uncertainty. He slowly settled into silence but kept his big scared eyes steady on hers.

She limped to the very middle, placing the majority of her weight on her left foot as she was favoring the right. Standing straight, she pivoted around in one spot, again counting the eleven boulders, but nothing happened.

"I'm here for my sister," she shouted, breaking the stillness of the glen. "A Faerie took her from our home in Castleblayney two days ago and I want her back." her young voice echoed back to her, but still no change.

"I have your baby!"

She waited, but still nothing happened. The changeling wriggled and fidgeted as she held him. Her little shoulders slumped and her bottom lip began to quiver. She wouldn't cry, she constrained herself, but she was so tired. Closing her eyes on the ensuing tears she hugged the baby tight, his angular little frame poked, but she still felt good to have him there.

As she turned to leave, feeling defeated, she sensed a change in the atmosphere around them. She stopped, straining her ears to hear anything, anything that was different. The silence in the circle was almost deafening, but she couldn't see anyone else around, even though she suddenly had this strange feeling they weren't alone anymore.

She felt the air oscillate and quiver as if a hummingbird just flitted by her right ear. She jerked; startled she peered around looking for whatever had buzzed by, when she felt another flap by her left.

Taken aback by the onslaught of flicks and flashes of an invisible attacker striking her face, she closed her eyes and started to run.

The blows followed her as she ran, the baby held firm against her chest, his sharp fingers dug into her skin as it held on and shrieked in fright. She couldn't tell where she was running, but whatever had ambushed her was growing. There seemed to be more and more and they hit her, hard.

She screamed as she was slapped from behind, then falling forward she was struck from the right and sent crashing to the ground. Taking the only defense she could, she curled up into a ball on her knees, her head tucked under her arms and the baby pinned beneath her body as she tried to protect it and as much of herself as she could from the assault.

Her heart beat so fast she wondered that it didn't just beat through her chest. Fear caused sweat to drip in huge drops from her forehead. She barely registered the frantic cries of the changeling over her own whimpering. Suddenly she detected the bursts of bluish haze in the periphery of her vision. It was then she realized she was seeing with her eyes closed, and these 'things' attacking her were faeries.

I guess we found them, she thought, but now what?

"Stop! Please just stop!" she screamed as loud as she could but it just seemed to urge them on.

She grimaced and curled into a tighter ball as she felt, and watched with her eyes closed, as they flew up into the air and dove down to pummel her back. There were dozens of them, and more and more seemed to be drawn to the scene, like a swarm of frenzied seagulls dive-bombing down into the water for their food then back up again.

She felt her consciousness start to slip away, her shirt was now torn and the skin on her back raw. Just as she was about to fall into blackness and blissful unawareness she heard the lilting sounds of flute music.

Through her light-headed daze she couldn't pin point exactly where the sound was coming from, but it grew stronger and louder until she could clearly make out the lively beat.

She then became aware that the bombarding against her back had stopped, she watched in her minds eye as the blue haze of the faeries drifted away from her and closer to the merry music.

Feeling brave enough, she opened her eyes and peeked through a crack between her arms and the ground, she could actually see the faeries now, which was new, she'd never seen them in their corporeal forms before. They were beautiful, she admitted. They looked just like humans only slightly shorter, and completely perfect, beautiful glowing skin, long flowing hair, they glided rather than walked and it was then she saw what they were walking towards.

A young girl faerie was the one making the music. She watched through her tiny peep hole as the young sprite danced along with the music she was blowing out of her set of wooden pan pipes. Her dark red, almost burgundy hair swung and swayed as she twisted and twirled. All the other faeries started to hum and sway and dance along with her.

Seeing her moment of escape, she snatched the changeling off the ground and ran, as fast as her little legs would carry her to the outer edge of the stone circle. The wind rushing past her ears as her legs pumped, drowned out the faeries' music, but she didn't slow, even as she burst out of the circle she didn't stop until someone grabbed hold of her arm, lurched her to a halt and dragged her, still clinging to the baby behind the cover of a tree.

A delicate hand was pressed firmly over her mouth to muffle her startled cry.

"It's okay, wee one, it's all right now." The soothing voice, thick with the accent of Ireland settled over her and calmed the pounding of her heart.

"I'm going to take my hand away from your mouth now, you have to be quiet."

She nodded her head to say she would, after she'd taken a big breath, her throat was parched and felt like sandpaper as she swallowed hard. She looked to the petite woman sitting beside her, she didn't need the flash of blue haze behind her eyes to tell her this woman was a faerie, her perfect complexion and the spangle in her big brown eyes gave it away.

The faerie bent her heart-shaped mouth into a radiant smile, "It'll be okay now." she repeated, her soft words comforting.

"Who are you?" the child managed to gasp between gulping in air.

"I'm Raisie."

"Are- are you one of them?" she inclined her head back at the stone circle where the faeries still danced to the young girl's music.

"Yes, I am part of the trooping faeries but we are not all the same. That child faerie playing the pipes is my daughter." Raisie turned her around by the shoulders so she could look at her back. "*Bocht leanbe, drochide-*" she spoke in Gaelic as she tsked over the ugly welts now risen over her skin and gently laid a cool hand over the sore marks and the pain instantly began to fade.

"Thank you." She smiled weakly at the older faerie, her breathing settling back to a normal pace.

"You're welcome." Raisie stroked a hand across her forehead and pushed the hair out her face. "We don't have much time, I know you are here looking for your sister."

"Is she here?"

Raisie tilted her head, sympathy clouding her eyes, "She was, but she is gone now. I'm sorry."

"What? Gone? Gone where?" Frantic now, she clutched the faerie's arm and jumped to her feet, Raisie glided up with her.

"I don't know where they took her, but all I can tell you is that trying to find her at this point, is a lost cause. She's probably not even in Ireland anymore. I'm so sorry wee one, I know you've traveled far and suffered much."

She'd cried so many tears in the last 48 hours it seemed there were no more left to shed. She knew what the faerie told her was true; deep down... she knew... it was too late.

She felt a gentle tugging on her pant leg and looked down at the changeling baby who was perched in the grass by her feet. Looking back up at Raisie she asked, "What about him?"

"Ah yes, the rejected one." Raisie turned her attention to the baby. She knelt down and held out her hands to him, but he wound his arms tighter around the young girls leg and turned his face away from the faerie woman. "I don't blame him for being a bit apprehensive of me, he's been through an ordeal too. I could never understand how a mother could discard their offspring just because of their appearance. It's such a shame too because he won't be this way forever." She smiled wistfully back at the girl, "If you – and he- would allow me, I'd like to take him as my own, I will give him a good home along with my daughter."

She was unsure whether to hand him over to this woman, seeing how scared he was and considering it was these faeries that had tossed him aside in the first place. Reading the uncertainty on her face, Raisie laid a reassuring hand on her shoulder, "Rest assured I will protect him, he will be safe and he will be loved."

Contemplating the soft, confiding eyes of the faerie she couldn't help but trust her, she felt this was the right thing to do, that she would look after the changeling; it's not like she could take care of him herself anyway. Crouching down she picked up the baby and hugged him to her chest, nestled his yellow face in the side of her neck.

"It'll be alright little buddy. This lady is gonna take care of you now, okay?" He screeched and yowled and fought to cling tighter to her neck. "No, no, now it's going to be alright, I promise you, please, shhh." She held him slightly away from her so she could look in his eyes, afraid his cries would draw the attention of the faeries still gathered inside the stone circle not too far away.

"Please, little guy just listen to me." He stopped thrashing in her arms and watched her with his big, black eyes, so trusting. "I wouldn't leave you with her if I wasn't sure she would take care of you, I know she will, just look at her and you'll see it too."

The baby shifted his gaze slightly to look at Raisie. They watched each other, seemed to communicate without speaking. A few seconds ticked by when the baby suddenly smiled and reached out to the faerie, she gathered him close in her arms.

"Well, I guess that's it for me, you take care little fella." She tapped the tip of his nose and turned to leave.

"Here, take this." Raisie handed her a small loaf of bread she pulled from the folds of her flowing dress, "You have a long walk home."

"Thanks." Smiling a weary, watery smile at the baby in parting, she walked away from them, the nimble notes of the pipe music drifted off behind her.

SHE WALKED ALL NIGHT, back through the woods, back towards home. The loaf of bread Raisie had given her had managed to keep her walking. Her legs felt like lead and every muscle screamed, but she was beyond feeling the pain. She was numb.

The sun had been up for a few hours by the time she reached the street her house was on, back in Castleblayney. She paused at the end of the road; there was Snuffles, Mrs. Flynn's little black poodle sleeping in the sunlight on her front stoop and Mr. O'Dell's green checkered mailbox, the bright red flag was standing straight up so the mailman must have been by already. It was then she noticed something was wrong, there was no signs of life anywhere, nobody out tending their gardens, even the two old ladies who usually met at the corner to gossip the day away were nowhere to be seen. It was then she saw the cloud of black smoke billowing up into the sky.

Her mind racing she gathered enough strength to jog down the street. *This can't be happening, oh please be all right, please be all right.* She tore around the bend in the street and stopped short when she saw the crowd of people gathered on the side of the road in front of her house. All at once she took in the big fire truck parked on the front lawn, the men in yellow suits and rubber boots were milling around, one was coiling up a huge white hose but her Mother was nowhere around. Then she saw the house, or what had been her house.

Shoving her way through the assembly of bystanders, she caught snippets of their conversations,

"…poor child…she doesn't even know yet …inside at the time… orphanage…Dublin…no living relatives…" she just kept walking toward the black sodden mess of fallen timbers and burning ashes. The world went fuzzy around her; only the house, burnt and broken was in focus.

She could smell the acrid stink the fire had left in the air, her nose burned from it. She fell to her knees; the grass was wet and soaked through her tattered pants.

She heard someone screaming, only later had she realized the screams were her own.

A woman dressed in a sharply tailored navy blue suit broke from the crowd and picked her way across the soggy lawn to where she knelt.

"Was this your home?" her voice sounded like it was coming from far away, but she caught the meaning and managed to nod when the woman crouched down beside her. "I'm sorry to have to tell you this, but apparently your mother was inside at the time of the fire, she… she didn't make it out in time." When the child didn't move or acknowledge that she had heard, the woman laid a hand on her shoulder, "Do you understand what I'm saying?" With still no response she tried a different tact, "I'm Ms. McCarthy, and I'm from Social Services, what's your name child?"

The girl lifted her face, tears streamed from her eyes leaving trails across her soot stained cheeks, "Cara. Cara Cahill."

Chapter 3

Durham, North Carolina, 2010

"...WHEN THEY HAD HEAPED UP *the barrow they went back again into the city, and being well assembled they held high feast in the house of Priam their king. Thus, then, did they celebrate the funeral of Hector tamer of horses."*

"Thank you Miss. Priest, you may take your seat." the professor instructed the girl as she finished reading. "And that concludes our study of Homers *Iliad*. So, questions? Comments?" He scanned the sea of young faces, and when no hands were raised he zeroed in on a blonde girl seated near the back who seemed more interested in her manicure than ancient mythology, "Miss. Donovan." The girl noticeably jumped at the call of her name. "What did you think about Achilles treatment of Hector's dead body?"

"What?" The girl flashed big brown eyes at him, clueless.

"You know, how he dragged Hector's dead and broken body behind his chariot back to his camp where he placed a river of animal blood around the corpse so the wild dogs and birds would devour it?" He watched her with patient eyes as she crinkled her noise as if there were a bad smell in the room.

"Eeeww, that is so gross."

His lips twitched as he fought back a smirk, "Yes, Miss. Donovan, I suppose it is." He glanced around the room once more and called on a young man in the middle row hiding behind the girl, at least he thought it was a girl, with the punked-up blue hair and spikes through her ears.

"Mr. Fulton, what did you think of the ending?"

"Well, to tell you the truth Professor Colby, it was kind of a let down."

"How so?" he inclined his head in question, the boy shifted in his seat.

"Well, we read all along about the war and the battles and stuff, which is cool, but then it comes down to Hector's death and it starts talking about how his family wants his body back."

"Uh-hum." he nodded in agreement.

"Well, then Achilles just folds and gives it to them." He leaned forward to peer around the blue head in front of him, "… I don't know, I guess I just expected it to end with a little bit more of a bang, it was anticlimactic."

"That's the word! Yes!" The professor jabbed a finger at the boy, "You hit it right on the head. It is anticlimactic." He jumped off the corner of his desk where he had been perched, skirted around it to write on the chalkboard behind.

He was a large man towering just under seven feet, he took care not to bang his hip on the side of the desk's shiny, oak top, his long legs tended to make him underestimate distances and his surprising strength always raised a few eye brows. One nudge of his hip would send the heavy desk skittering across the room, but that's just part of being a werewolf.

He slid an already used chalkboard up into the wall to reveal a clean one underneath; he spoke as he rapidly scribbled notes. "We can call the end of this poem anticlimactic because it isn't really the end of the story. The Trojan war wages for ten years, we are at year nine." He turned briefly back to face the class, "I'm sure all of you know the outcome of this story without ever having read it, or without ever having seen Brad Pitt portray it on the big screen." Snickers of laughter rippled through the student body as he turned back to the board to continue writing.

"Since Homer's audience is already acquainted with the outcome, as are we, it seems fitting not to end the poem with the ending of the war, but, rather with the ending of the main conflict, that being Achilles' anger." He punctuated his statement with dotting a period on the chalkboard and wiped the dust off his hands, leaving smears of white over his brown slacks.

He rarely deviated from his usual attire of brown trousers, crisp white shirt, buttoned up to the second last button before his stiffly starched collar; the top button would never close due to the considerable girth of his neck. He never wore a tie because of this anomaly but always had a tweed blazer, some even equipped with suede patches on the elbows.

"Achilles has been portrayed throughout the entire poem as prideful, selfish, impulsive; quite temperamental actually, and his rage is a key driving force to the whole story." He pulled the metal chair out from under his desk and took a seat, the spring groaning from his weight as he spread his legs straight out so they'd fit under the desk. "So it makes sense to end with the original conflict resolved, because the end of the war is really inconsequential, the outcome is held in the hands of the gods."

"Then why do they even bother fighting a war?" a student called out.

"Where would mankind be if we never fought against our fate?" He smiled absently to no one in particular, "We all believe in free will and that we make our own futures, but assume for a moment there is some cosmic power out there whom decides where our life will lead and if that path is not where we want to go, wouldn't you fight to change it?"

"I don't know Professor, it seems futile somehow."

He peered out the window, the noon sun hung high in the sky, "I guess some of us think it wouldn't be worth living a life if we couldn't make a difference in it." The silence in the room stretched for a moment or two as each and all seemed to reflect in their own thoughts, until he turned his attention back to the class.

"And that brings us to the essay assignment. I want you to discuss Homer's portrayal of the gods, and their relationship with humans… and their fate. Fifteen hundred words, double spaced, I want it by Friday."

The students began to gather their belongings to leave, "Two weeks from now when we return from spring break, we'll be starting our study of Homer's *Odyssey*, please be prepared, I've ordered more copies, you can purchase them in-" The professor was cut short just as the entire classroom started to shake.

Gasps and startled screams rang throughout the room, chairs and desks scraped across the floor as the building vibrated, books tumbled off of shelves, people scrambled to find an exit and everyone tried to jam through the door at once.

Professor Colby leapt from his seat and grimaced when he rapped his knees on the edge of the desk, causing it to tilt, it would have flipped over if he hadn't slammed his hands down on it to keep it upright.

"People! Remain calm!" he shouted over the din of the windowpanes banging in their frames.

It amazed him how useless all those earthquake drills they hold in elementary school appear to be when faced with the real situation.

His loud voice broke through the hysteria of the students, and they stopped struggling to squeeze through the door. He could smell their fear, a sweet, musky scent that tingled up his nose and tried to muddle his brain.

The wolf instincts urged him to advance, his pulse raced at the anticipation of attack and chaos, but he ruthlessly tamped it down.

Eight years ago when he had decided to take this position as a Professor of Classical Studies at Duke University, he felt he had sufficient control over his more aptly named, *animal* urges, or else he would never had let himself work with humans.

But Duke had appealed to both sides of him, to his erudite scholarly side with its ancient gothic architecture and culture, and to his animalistic side with its lush grounds and robust scenery, it tugged at the wolf in him whom longed to run, to frolic, to hunt. Everyday the smells called to him, but he had learned to control the yearning, as he did so now.

"There is no need to panic, if you'll all stop and take notice, you'll see the quaking has stopped, it was only a slight tremor." He deliberately started to breath through his mouth and calmed his heart rate from jackrabbit speed to a steady thumping.

He heard their muffled sighs of relief as the students, slightly embarrassed, looked at each other and commenced gathering their dropped books and pencils.

"It isn't often we have an earthquake here in North Carolina, but it is not abnormal to periodically experience land tremors." He righted the tipped over mug on his desk and picked up a stack of papers that was now dripping with the leftovers of yesterday's coffee, by its corners and shook it over the cup when the air was pierced by a loud croaking shriek. It resonated around the atmosphere like the sound of a piano string being plucked.

His head snapped up at the sound, wide-eyed he looked out the window; birds in the trees took to flight, as they were startled.

"What was that?"

"I don't know. Some kind of freaky bird maybe?"

The student's voices sounded dull and far away in his head.

It can't be. It's impossible.

"Professor Colby, are you alright?" the young girl standing in front of his desk jolted slightly as he flashed his frozen gold eyes on her,

"It was a raven's cry." He didn't even register who she was or what she'd said as he spoke. He grabbed his green tweed jacket off the back of his chair, the force of the motion as he flicked it over his arm sent the metal chair pitching sideways till it smashed into the wall and fell over with a clatter, but he didn't notice.

He pushed his way through the cluster of students who stood statue still as they watched him in bemusement.

He flew out of the classroom and headed at a quick jog to the staircase, he wove down the three floors in the Allen building, his brown leather loafers slapping against the stone steps as he skipped three stairs in every stride.

Once in the lobby he made a b-line for the doors and burst out into the warm March afternoon. Turning left he made his way to the parking lot, throwing his jacket on as he ran.

When he reached his aging Subaru Forester, he folded himself into the driver's seat and fumbled with the keys as he tried, unsuccessfully, to get them into the ignition. Taking a deep breath he made his hands slow down and focused, he managed to get the car started, it roared to life and bucked backwards as he shifted into reverse then stuttered forward as he clumsily switched gears.

"Come on baby, don't die on me." He pleaded anxiously with the engine as he slammed on the gas and the vehicle coughed a cloud of exhaust then took off like a bullet.

His tires squealed as he turned a sharp right out of the parking lot and shot down Flower Drive. He entered the dreaded roundabout and missed the exit for Campus Drive in his haste; cursing himself he went around the circle again and cut off a car behind him to get off on the right street.

At a speed he would never consider safe to travel he wound his way under the Durham freeway and maneuvered through the triangle of streets until he turned onto Morgan Street. Winging passed the stately

Carolina Theatre he wedged his clunky SUV in between two parked cars on the side of the road and jumped out, he hadn't bothered with a seat belt, although normally he would have, but just this one time he figured he could forego it, it's not like a car crash could kill him anyway.

He owned the small brick building right off the sidewalk; it stretched two stories up, tall and narrow. The top two floors he used as his apartment, which he shared with two other werewolves, the bottom was a used bookstore they'd taken over when he'd bought the place.

He took the front steps in one leap, burst through the bookstore doors and headed to the back where another set of stairs led up to the apartment.

"Hey Caleb, you're home early." He didn't even hear that Oliver, who was manning the bookstore, had spoken to him, just rushed up the stairs and into the apartment.

OLIVER HAD A TWIN brother Spike, not identical in any way but two closer siblings Caleb had never seen than Spike and Oliver.

Spike sat on the orange, threadbare sofa they'd picked up at a thrift store, watching The Price is Right and eating the first of three Big Mac's he had on the coffee table in front of him.

"Hey man, can you believe this show without Bob Barker? I mean seriously, it's sacrilege." Spike watched Caleb run into the next room without even a glance in his direction. He hauled himself up off the couch to follow him just as Oliver came into the apartment.

"What's up?" Spike asked his brother.

"Dunno, came tearing through the bookstore, didn't say a word."

They both walked into the small room Caleb used as his office/ library, the walls were lined with shelves that were overflowing with books, which Caleb was now pulling out at random.

'Where is it? Where is it?" he muttered as he searched through the hundreds of books he'd collected over the years on mythology and ancient history.

"What's he gibbering about?" Spike asked as he took another huge bite out of his burger. Oliver shrugged and watched Caleb tear around the room like a whirling dervish, books flying left and right, pages scattering as they beat against the walls.

"Ah hah! Here it is." he exclaimed. He hefted the large leather tome off of the shelf and slammed it down on the desk that took up most of the room. Flipping wildly through the pages, dust fanned up, Oliver sneezed as he and Spike came to stand behind him and peered over his shoulder.

Caleb trailed a finger across the rows of words as he read out loud in a foreign language and ran his other hand through his sandy brown hair that kept falling into his eyes. His wavy locks were always too long, being a werewolf his hair grew inordinately fast, and unlike Spike and Oliver who routinely buzzed their heads military style, he put off getting it cut until it was brushing his shoulders and it was noticeably in the way.

"This is it!" he exclaimed.

"What's it?" Oliver asked, bewildered and a bit nervous at seeing Caleb so erratic.

"Did you guys feel the earthquake earlier?"

"Yah."

"Of course."

"And did you hear the ravens cry?"

"A raven?"

"Was that what that was?"

"Here just listen." Caleb's voice was excited but strained as he translated the book aloud.

"Brothers will fight and kill each other,
Sisters, children.
It is harsh in the world.
-An axe age, a sword age
-Shields are riven-
A wind age, a wolf age-"

"A wolf age? I like the sound of that." Spike quipped but was silenced with one look from Caleb before he continued reading.

"The earth will quake on a raven's mournful cry
-All hell has broken free-
Before the world goes headlong,
No man will have mercy on another."

Caleb kept his eyes on the page as silence fell, as if he was looking for something else, anything else that would negate what he'd just read.

"What does that mean?" Oliver asked Spike who didn't seem too concerned with how freaked Caleb was acting; it took a lot to faze his brother though.

"I don't know, it's all Greek to me. Hah! You get it?" Spike snorted a laugh around a mouthful of Big Mac and jabbed Oliver in the stomach with his elbow. "Greek?"

Oliver shot him a withering look as he rubbed the sore spot the shot had left on his ribs.

"It's not Greek, it's Scandinavian." Caleb turned to look at them then, his face grim, the jaunty theme song from the game show on the TV in the other room played dully in the background, "It means Ragnarok is coming. – The end of the world."

Chapter 4

CALEB SAT IN THE BACK seat of a New York taxi, wedged between Spike and Oliver. His long legs were bent and propped up against the plastic partition separating passengers and driver; his knees almost touched his chin. Oliver was quiet, not abnormally so, he rarely had much to say; he watched with apparent detachment at the scenery whipping by outside his window. Spike on the other hand had nodded off to the muffled sounds of AC/DC beating out of his headphones, the guy could sleep anywhere.

It had been a long eight hours since the scene back in his office in North Carolina. Once he'd read the passage about the earth quaking on a raven's cry he knew what was coming, what had happened, and who he had to talk to.

But just deciding to pick up and travel somewhere on the spur of the moment was easier said than done for a werewolf.

After he'd regained his composure and told the twins he needed to get to New York ASAP, he'd spent forty-five minutes trying to get the New York City Alpha wolf on the phone.

His name was Desmond Ackley; he's been the Alpha wolf in New York for the past twenty-five years. His territory encompasses all of New York State, up through Maine, over to Toronto and down around Virginia. His pack is one of the largest in the world with thirty-two members whereas most packs are a family of seven to eight werewolves.

The most dangerous predator to a werewolf are most often a rival pack and a werewolf should never enter another pack's territory without express permission from the Alpha, unless of course they have a death wish, which the other pack will be more than happy to see come true.

FOR CALEB, PACK POLITICS had always been a pill of discord, one that was bitter to swallow. Originally a pack is started by two werewolves and their offspring but over time as old members die and new members join the name of 'family' becomes more of an honorary title than a reality. Throughout history, these families evolved into elite fraternities whose initiation rituals make college hazing look like preschoolers play.

It was one of the reasons why Caleb had left his pack and struck out on his own. He'd wandered the countryside, keeping a low profile when passing through territories and had finally settled in Durham; oddly enough the city wasn't a part of any other packs domain.

"Hey Caleb."

"Huh?" Caleb craned his neck to peer at Oliver.

"How much longer do we have?"

Caleb went to look at his wristwatch but found his hand was jammed between his legs and the partition, he glanced at the taxi's dashboard clock, it blinked six o'clock PM underneath a swinging pair of red, fuzzy dice and a beaded rosary.

"Eleven hours and counting."

"I guess twenty-four hours was too much to ask for." Oliver turned back to look out the window.

Caleb had sworn he'd never be part of a pack again, but months after he'd fled, Spike and Oliver showed up on his doorstep; he'd assumed they were sent to kill him for deserting but instead they'd wanted to join him and they've been loyal to him ever since. Even though Caleb didn't consider the three of them a pack, he knew that the brothers looked upon him as their Alpha and would lay down their lives for him, a thought not altogether comforting.

CALEB CLENCHED HIS TEETH as the cab bounced down the pot-holed street, his left leg was beginning to tingle from the lack of circulation and wondered how much farther it was to Brooklyn.

When he'd finally managed to talk to Desmond Ackley and wriggle his way through all the tact and decorum needed to charm an Alpha, he'd gained authorization to enter the New York territory for fifteen hours, not a second longer; Mr. Ackley had been quite adamant on what would happen should they overstay their welcome.

Thinking back on the conversation, Caleb was impressed with the elaborate song and dance he'd performed to gain admittance to the territory without letting on the reason why.

Finally, when it seemed the thirty-minute cab ride from JFK Airport to Brooklyn would last forever, the bright yellow car pulled over to the side of the street, next to a row of Brownstone houses.

"This is it, 613 Carroll Street." the taxi driver shouted over his shoulder at them.

Oliver stepped out on the sidewalk, and scanned the neighborhood, ears perked to every sound, and nostrils flaring slightly as he sniffed for any sign of a threat nearby. Even having permission to be there, didn't mean they should let their guard down.

Oliver bent down and stuck his head back into the cab, "All clear."

"Spike." Caleb nudged the sleeping figure next to him.

"Wha?!" The cab rocked back and forth as Spike jolted his huge bulk out of sleep, snapping to attention he wrapped his forehead against the seat in front of him, "Son of a ... urgh!" he wiped a beefy hand across his face and glared at Caleb, "there's something sticky on that. Well... there was, it's all over my face now."

Caleb just grinned, "We're here." He unfolded his legs to wedge his way out the car door.

"Gross." Spike grumbled as he climbed out.

The taxi drove away as the three of them stood on the sidewalk and turned to face the row of brownstone townhouses that lined the busy street.

"This the place?" Oliver asked Caleb.

"I don't know. I've never been here, but this was her last known address."

"Only one way to find out." Spike shoved passed them and started up the crumbling front stairs and yanked open the heavy wooden doors leading into the building,

Caleb and Oliver exchanged an amused look then started up the stairs after him.

Inside, the foyer was dim, the last of the dying sunlight struggled through the dirty windowpanes. The air smelled almost sickeningly sweet of baked apple wafting from the French patisserie next door.

Against the right wall rose a large staircase carved out of solid oak, now scuffed from decades of use, that lead to the apartment on the second level. To the left was a door, it was slightly ajar and painted a deep purple. Caleb moved toward it and smelled the flowery fragrance of burning incense even though it was hard to tell next to the overwhelming smells from the bakery. "This is her place." He stepped in front of the door and lifted his fist to knock when a woman's voice beckoned from within, "Come in Caleb, I've been waiting for you."

He faced the twins hovering behind him, meeting their stunned expressions. They shifted in front of him, nudging him back, "You better let us go first." Oliver suggested and walked through the open door before him. The brothers' protective measures, though he'd assured them that they were unnecessary, had become a habit. Caleb stepped up between the two brothers who had stopped a few feet into the room and were watching the woman who stood in the middle of it. She was in her late fifties, her grey hair long and curly down her rigid back, her eyes a pale blue, rimmed in dusky purple eye shadow, she shifted her gaze from one werewolf to the next then back to Caleb.

"Lucille. It's good to see you." Caleb greeted her.

The corners of her thin line of a mouth lifted in a smile as she came forward and clasped him around the waist in a hug, her head barely reaching his chest, he had to stoop to return the embrace.

"It has been a very long time, too long." She stepped back, her cluster of bracelets clinked on her arms she tilted her head back to get a closer look at him. "You look well." She decided after a moment's scrutiny, "Still growing taller are you? Or maybe I'm shrinking. Either way you seem to grow a foot every time we meet."

"Lucille, I hate to get right down to the point but we've come here for your help and it appears you were expecting us."

"Yes. I assumed after today's events I would be getting a visit from you." She glanced over at the grandfather clock, ticking away in the corner, "You do work fast don't you." She smiled and peered around him, "And I see you've brought your little werewolf friends along. Good, good."

Caleb signaled for Spike not to say anything when he could sense his irritation mounting. "So the tremor was felt here as well then?"

"Hmm, all over the world I assume."

"So does it mean what I think it means?"

"I'm afraid I can't say just yet, we are a few members short." Lucille strolled leisurely across the room and lowered herself onto a plush leather sofa.

"What do you mean? It's just us three coming." Caleb asked. But Lucille didn't reply, she arranged the silky folds of her dress more comfortably around her and placed a veined hand delicately on her crossed knee.

"You're expecting someone else?" Caleb moved over the Persian rug and sat across from her in a rickety rocking chair. "Who?" She smiled serenely but remained silent. Resigned that she wasn't about to say anything more until whom ever she expected to arrive did so, Caleb sat back in the chair and waited.

Twenty minutes ticked by, the grandfather clock bonged the half hour and still no one had spoken and no one else had come. Having lost patience with the old lady's tactics Spike commenced pacing the floor. "This is ridiculous!" he stormed.

"Just be patient." Caleb instructed.

"Patient for what? Look lady!" he stomped over to stand in front of Lucille, "we flew all the way over here because Caleb thought you could help us figure out what was going on with this whole earthquake/raven thing, so if you don't know anything, why don't you just say so and stop wasting our time?" She met his irate ranting with another coy smile but still said nothing. Throwing his arms into the air in frustration he marched over to an opening in the wall that lead to another room and leaned his shoulder against the doorframe, crossed his arms over his chest and sulked. He glared over at the old woman again; she was observing him with a smug expression, almost as if she could read the thoughts running through his head.

Old bag, I could snap you like a twig. He clenched his fists tighter. He glanced at Caleb, still sitting quietly, rocking back and forth in the chair and gazing out into space. *I guess if Cal doesn't mind waiting, I don't either. But damn it, this is so useless! Anyone can see the old hag is having us on.* He sneered when he saw the old woman still smiling at him and turned his attention to his brother who was standing sentry, looking out the window at the traffic on the street below, his hands in his pockets.

That's Ollie for ya; he's got patience down to the marrow. As he watched his brother he recognized the moment his stance went from relaxed to tense. Spike quickly went and stood beside him, "What is it?" he spoke softly so as not to alarm anyone.

Oliver didn't take his eyes off the window even though every muscle in his body quivered "Vampires. Two of them. They're coming into the building."

Spike whirled around as he heard a noise at the door. Two men stood in the doorway, "We're looking for Lucille Callaway." the taller of the two said.

Lucille stood up from her place on the sofa, "Now we may begin."

IN A SINGLE BOUND Spike and Oliver were across the room and in front of Caleb. "You didn't say we were waiting for vampires." Spike spat at Lucille.

"Would you have stayed if I had?" she asked sweetly. Ignoring the death glares aimed at her from the twins she walked over to the new guests. "Welcome, I am Lucille. And we have been waiting for you."

The man who had spoken surveyed the scene before him, two snarling werewolves who were obviously trying to guard their Alpha wasn't a scenario he'd planned to deal with. Removing his hand from the pocket of his black leather jacket he shook the old woman's hand but kept his eyes on the werewolves. Lucille followed his gaze and signed, "Caleb, would you please call off your watchdogs, these men aren't going to hurt you."

The tall vampire watched as man rose from his seat behind the two defending wolves, he stood a whole head above them. "Stand down boys."

At Caleb's command the brothers reluctantly stepped aside but remained close to his side as he walked toward the vampires.

Caleb offered a hand to the lead vampire and smiled reassuringly, "My name is Caleb Colby and I'm assuming we're both here for the same reason."

"I'm Beckett Graham, this is Gannon Dempsey." He took Caleb's hand in a firm handshake and nodded his head at the man in the doorway behind him as an introduction. "I'm here for some answers."

"You sure you can trust them, Beck?" The vampire names Gannon whispered into Becketts ear.

"Trust us?" Spike advanced on the vampires, "We're not some leech

32

who'll suck the blood out of you for his next meal." Spike and Gannon had moved toe-to-toe, muscles straining as they faced off.

"I've never been fond of the taste of mange so don't worry you're pretty little head about it, Fido."

"Gannon!" The sharp tone in Beckett's voice had both men easing back.

"I think we can set aside this centuries old feud for a few moments and get down to what we really came here for." Caleb advised them all and turned to Beckett, who nodded in agreement.

All eyes turned to Lucille who was waiting patiently in the doorway to the adjoining room, "So, if you boys all agree to play nicely, you may come into the study and I'll tell you all I can about what you want to know." With that she turned on her heel and left them to follow her.

Beckett looked at Caleb and shrugged, "Might as well hear what she has to say." He motioned for Gannon to come as he walked after Lucille, the werewolves followed.

Chapter 5

THE STUDY WAS REALLY THE dining room, a small paneled room off of the tidy white kitchen. The walls were lined with shelves; a few books adorned them but were mostly crowded with tiny, coloured glass bottles, different bowls of crystals, satchels of powders, thick candles and dried herbs hanging from hooks screwed into the underside of a shelf.

Instead of a dining table there was a round coffee table draped with a purple velvet cloth, marked with golden astrological symbols. It sat about a foot off the floor, surrounded by bright red pillows. Lucille was sitting Indian style on one of the pillows, hands clasped on the table in front of her.

"Take a seat gentlemen."

"You've got to be kidding me." Spike complained when he saw the pillows. Caleb sent him a warning look and proceeded to sit down across from Lucille. With a not too subtle sigh Spike knelt down next to him, Oliver followed suit. Beckett took the cushion to Caleb's right then looked back at the door where Gannon still stood.

"I'll stand thanks." He settled back against the wall and crossed his ankles.

"Alright, the other bloodsucker doesn't want to play so what now lady? We gonna join hands and sing kumbaya together?" Lucille fixed Spike with a bland look.

"I'll assume by that statement that Caleb hasn't seen fit to tell you who I am or why he came to see me." She looked at each person seated around the table, noticeably excluding Gannon.

"And Beckett, we've never met but since you've sought me out, is it safe to assume you know what I do?" She addressed Beckett and waited for his nod in agreement.

"Well then, for those of you who don't know, I am a Medium." she paused for emphasis.

"What does your size have to do with anything?" Spike asked, confused.

Gannon snickered from behind them and Caleb placed a restraining hand on Spike's arm before he tore at the vampire.

"What she means, is she is a Spirit Operator. She communicates with the spirit world." Caleb explained, his firm voice carrying the command to stay calm.

"That's right," she confirmed.

"So what? You see dead people?" Oliver asked.

"No, I can't see any of them but I can hear them and they aren't all dead people. Some of them are the spirits of the departed, yes, but some are spirits of the earth, some are angelic entities…"

"Whoa! You're saying you talk to angels?" Spike held up a hand to interrupt and she smiled softly.

"Only on very rare occasions do the heavenly messengers decide to speak to me."

"Okay, so how is a dead guy or a spirit from a tree or something going to help us figure out if the world is coming to an end? Do they know the future or something?"

"Spirits aren't bound by the same limitations as we are, they can travel through time, dimensions, and see things and know things we could never even imagine." Lucille shifted her weight more comfortably on the cushion and spread her hand over the soft tablecloth.

"Of course the spirits are limited in what they can reveal to the human world, hence the reason I can't pick the winning lottery numbers every week." she winked at Caleb and continued, "There are quite a few of us out there who have a natural aptitude to commune with the spirits but through certain… spiritual enhancement … shall we say, that can help us reach the more intangible beings, and can help us communicate with them, you see, generally a medium can only hear the spirits but rarely speak back."

"When we last met, you were only hearing the voices. Are you saying you've discovered a way to speak back?" Caleb queried, leaning closer to the table.

"Yes, Caleb, I have." She watched him as he sat back again, stunned. "All these things you see around us." she waved her arms to encompass the room, "All the trappings of spiritualism, astrology and even some of witchcraft, when used properly can enhance the ability. Do you remember the number of this building?"

"613." Beckett answered.

"That's right." She beamed at him like a Kindergarten teacher pleased with her pupil. "I knew this place was the one I had been searching for my whole life." She turned her attention back to Caleb, "When we met almost nine years ago, we were both searching for a place meant just for us, well this was mine." She pulled a deck of cards out of the folds in her dress; they were worn and torn around the edges. "Don't worry these aren't tarot cards." she assured Oliver when she noticed him squirm uneasily. She flipped the top card face up on the table; on it was a golden pentacle on a background of starbursts of reds, greens, whites and purples. "This is the symbol for the number six, its ruler is the planet Venus, and it represents harmony, balance, serenity and truth." Flipping over another card she placed it in line next to the other one, all eyes turned to see what this one was.

"This is number one, guarded by the sun, it stands for positive and pure energy. And lastly," flipping another card on the table, "this is number three, the infamous Mars."

"What does that stand for?" Beckett asked as he examined the intricate drawing of a flaming triangle with a single eye in its center that was painted on the card.

"Mars governs magic and intuition. But most importantly right now, Mars will help us find the spirits who can tell us what we need to know about the future. The number three is a time identifier, having a finger so to speak, in the past, the present, and the future."

She stood up from her seat on the floor, with more ease than one would imagine a women of her age could possess, and went to the shelves on the wall behind her.

While her back was turned, Beckett leaned closer to Caleb, "You believing all of this?"

"I like to keep an open mind about most things." he replied in a hushed tone. "Why did you come to her if you don't believe in what she does?"

He thought for a moment, as if debating how much to say. "I heard she was the best."

"At fortune telling?"

"At getting answers."

They turned away from each other again as Lucille returned to the table. Before she sat again she shook her closed fist over the purple cloth and sprinkled a fine white powder in the shape of a triangle. She dusted her hands over the floor then placed a smooth green aventurine gem on each of the triangle's corners and finally, she positioned a thick red candle in the center and lit it with a long wooden match.

"The triangle, representing the three ages of Mars, the aventurine stone for luck and the red candle, to harness energy."

Taking her seat again she leaned closer to the table and closed her eyes. "I'm going to begin now, I'll need absolute silence. It will take me a few moments to find the right spirits who will be the most helpful." She closed her eyes, lifted her hands and began wafting the red smoke that was floating up from the candles wick and took deep breaths of its heady scent.

The group around the table watched in silence. Lucille lifted her arms over her head; her face titled up and raised her voice, loud and clear as she spoke.

"Oh elevated spirits of the other realm, heed my call, move among us and commune with me." As soon as the words left her mouth the candle flame shot in a towering column to the ceiling, they all jumped back except for Lucille, who lowered her arms.

"Is this normal?" Beckett asked, he held a hand up close to the flame and felt the heat billowing from it.

"I don't know, I've never seen her work before, but she doesn't seem too concerned." Caleb shot a glance at the twins; they were tense, muscles taut, and ready to jump into action in case something went wrong. He saw that Gannon was no longer leaned nonchalantly against the wall but stood rail straight, eyes fixed on the flame.

Lucille's head was twitching, left, right, up then down in sporadic little jerks, like she was trying to focus on a darting fly. Then she stopped, her head cocked to the right, "No, you are not who I am looking for."

Everyone looked at the empty space next to her into which she seemed to be speaking.

"There's no one there." Spike observed sounding a little nervy.

"No one *we* can see." Caleb followed Lucille's fitful movements as she went back to searching.

They went through the similar routine three more times until Lucille startled them by shouting, "You! You're the one I am looking for. Please, won't you help us?"

Her audience watched her expectantly as she finally opened her eyes, blinked to adjust to the light shimmering off the spear of flame from the candle. "It's agreed to answer some questions."

"Okay, well, ask him if the earthquake and the raven's cry actually mean that Ragnarok is coming?" Caleb said.

Lucille asked the question out loud to the vacant space to her left and waited.

"Yes. It says the events leading up to the final battle have been set in motion, the end of the world is coming."

Caleb expelled the breath he'd been holding in one long whoosh. "So the legend is true."

"Apparently so." Lucille confirmed.

"Has Loke been released? Ask the it, please." Caleb ran a not too steady hand through his hair while she relayed the message.

"Yes. The earth quakes as the gates of hell break open and all the prisoners of its deepest fathoms are released on a raven's cry."

Beckett sighed in frustration, "How does the spirit know that?"

"It says it has seen; it knows what will happen and how this ends."

"But how do you know it's not just some guy that knows a lot about ancient mythology? I mean, we all know how the story goes," Beckett looked around at the others, "Well, at least Caleb and I know how it goes, but how can we know for sure this being *really* knows that it's all true?"

"Good point." Caleb interjected.

Lucille suddenly jerked; her body vibrated violently then her spine snapped straight.

"Lucille?" Caleb reached across the table to grab her arm; he could feel it quiver under his touch. Her pupils swiveled back into her head and she fixed him with a blank white stare that had him dropping his hand.

"You doubt my word?" Lucille spoke but the sound wasn't her voice, it was deep and far off.

"Hey man, I think it's in her." Spike lurched to his feet, "What should I do?" he shouted.

"You will do nothing." the spirit spoke through Lucille. "You want my help? Then listen up!" Spike moved closer in behind Caleb, Oliver stood up next to him.

"Then start talking." Spike warned the thing that had taken over Lucille's body.

Lucille's neck cracked uncomfortably as the spirit craned her head from side to side as if it were trying to work out a kink. "Thousands of millennium ago, demons wandered the netherworld, giants lived in mountains, and gods ruled the skies and governed the lives of you mere mortals here on earth."

"Mere mortals? Who the does he think he is?" Spike asked, affronted.

"Maybe he's an angel." Beckett muttered, his eyes glued to Lucille's slack face. Spike considered that and decided to shut up.

"Besides, I wouldn't say anybody in this room would be considered completely human." Caleb added.

The spirit shifted Lucille's white eyes from person to person, seeing they were listening, and continued.

"Loke the trickster, born of two giants, witted his way into the god's realm, destined to lead the evil forces against the gods in the final fight of Ragnarok. When his misdeeds and malicious antics were carried too far, the kingdom of the divine fell, the age of the gods ended, and the age of vampires and werewolves on earth began.

Although the gods were no more, and Loke and his evil were enslaved in hell for eternity, Ragnarok would still come to pass."

"Loke is now free, he hides on the earth, and he searches for something that will secure his victory. The war is coming, he gathers his army, and you have been lead here to do the same. The races must unite, against all odds. The battle will be fought or earth will be lost."

With these last words, Lucille cried out and her body wrenched backward at an impossible angle, convulsed once, her eyes rolled forward and she slumped forward, limp. The spirit was gone.

BECKETT LEAPT FROM HIS seat and ran to Lucille's side. He lifted her head off her chest and felt for a pulse. "She's fine, just passed out." He looked at Gannon who had edged farther out the door, "Go get some water!" he ordered. "Now!" he yelled when he didn't move.

Caleb took her limp hand in his enormous one and gently rubbed the pressure point on her wrist. Gannon brought in a glass of water and handed it to Beckett who sprinkled a few drops on Lucille's dry lips.

Slowly her eyes fluttered open; she moaned and placed a shaky hand on her forehead. "It possessed me."

"We know. Come on, let's get you onto the couch." He carefully lifted her as if she were a child; she seemed old now and unbearably frail.

"That was a first for me. Can't say I liked it either." Caleb carried her back into the living room and softly placed her on the sofa. She drained the glass of water Beckett had handed to her. "I'll be alright." she smiled weakly and patted Caleb's arm in reassurance.

"Lucille, did you hear what it said?" Caleb asked as he crouched next to her.

"Well of course I heard, it was in me." He grinned; glad she was sounding more like herself. She looked around at all the faces hovering over her and then back at Caleb, "I'm sorry it was kind of cryptic, but the spirit was only allowed to reveal so much of the future; but it did say something else in my head, just before it left me."

"What?" Beckett asked.

She laid her head back on the arm of the sofa as if it was too heavy to hold up any longer. "It said you need to find a woman, she will help you find the rest of the answers you seek. Her name is Cara Cahill." She sighed and closed her eyes.

"Lucille?" Caleb prodded gently. "How do we find this woman?"

"If you look for her, you will find her. That's your blessing... but her curse." she said, her voice barely a whisper before she drifted off to sleep.

Chapter 6

County Mayo, Ireland, 2000

"LETS STOP HERE A MOMENT, shall we?" Cara called over her shoulders. To an untrained eye one might think she was speaking to no one at all, but a moment later a little man, no higher than a milking stool came tromping out of the brush.

"If you need a break, I guess this place is good as any." The leprechaun fussed ill temperedly.

"Come now Ferris, park your wee bottom under a tree for a moment and have a rest." she smiled as he crossed his short arms and stuck out his bearded chin like a defiant child and plopped to the ground where he stood in front of her.

"Suit yourself." She pulled a canteen out of her leather sack and took a gulp of water; she didn't bother offering any to Ferris, as she knew he'd refuse.

She lowered herself to the ground and leaned back against a tree and enjoyed the quiet forest noises, at least the ones she could hear over the sound of Ferris' grinding teeth.

"The air has been getting colder these past few weeks." she observed as she took a deep breath into her lungs and shivered from the refreshing chill. She ignored Ferris' derisive snort.

"The children will have to wear a coat under their costumes on Halloween next week."

"Ah jeez, don't say you're after telling those woeful stories again about your own all-hallows eves as a child." Ferris groaned and rolled his eyes.

"Why Ferris, I didn't realize you'd been listening." She grinned at having caught him up. She fingered the silver chain around her neck, a small Celtic cross pendant hung gently from it.

"Well I'd have to be near deaf not to catch *some* of your ramblings now wouldn't I?" He jumped to his feet and stomped back into the cover of the brush.

Cara was accustomed to Ferris' cantankerous ways; he was a persnickety little curmudgeon, but what leprechaun isn't? She'd found him, or more accurately, he'd found her, four years ago. It was near impossible to find a leprechaun; they're sneaky little bastards, cavorting about the countryside as they do. It's been said that if a person was to catch a leprechaun in their gaze, he was held to that spot and would not be able to get away, but in one blink he'd be gone forever. Of course no other human has ever been lucky enough to see one to prove this theory true or false, but many a soul has tried, and once a leprechaun's been caught, he is forced to bestow good luck upon you.

Cara chuckled to herself as she thought back to the day four years ago when she and Ferris had crossed paths. She'd run away from the St. Francis Orphanage in Dublin when she was only thirteen, she couldn't stay in that place any longer. Since that day in Castleblayney when she'd watched her house burn to the ground with her mother inside, she'd been determined to find out what was happening to her. While the other children were out playing hopscotch and red rover, Cara had hidden herself in the cleaning closet of the orphanage and focused on her *other* sight. She crinkled her nose as she remembered the harsh smell of chemicals like it were yesterday.

Whenever she closed her eyes she saw another world, one that lived amongst ours, made of all the imaginary creatures that mothers told cautionary tales about to make their children behave. They were invisible to everyone else, but when she closed her eyes and focused, she could see them, silhouettes of their shapes, glowing in a hazy color, each species having a different hue: fairies a pale blue, leprechauns a yellowy green, banshees misty grey, and eventually she was able to tell them apart.

She remembered feeling so special at having been given this gift, to be allowed to see the wonderful things that everyone else could only dream of and wonder about, until she discovered there was a dark side to her talent.

Soon she realized that every creature she could sense within a two hundred mile radius would inevitably come to her. She would be running from malicious fairies in the schoolyard, terrorized by the Dullahan, tramping around on his huge black steed and swinging his severed head by its hair, and woke up numerous mornings with her hair twisted into such vicious elf locks. She recalled sobbing and wondering why this was happening to her, as the furious head mistress ruthlessly cut the knots out of her hair, leaving her nearly bald.

Then she thought back to when she and the changeling baby were in the stone circle years earlier and every faerie from miles seemed to be attacking her. She realized then that they were drawn to her, as if she were some faerie beacon.

She understood then that if she stayed in any one place too long, every creature within miles would find her, so she left; packed up the two changes of clothes she owned and headed out on her own.

A few days after her flight from Dublin she'd found herself at a crossroads out in the country. She couldn't say where she was exactly but she'd been avoiding people and had been cutting across fields and meadows, and scampering along the low stonewalls that bisected the landscape until she ended up in farm land. She stopped in the center of the dirt road and turned herself full circle trying to decide which way to go.

When she turned to the west she saw him, there was Ferris just strolling down the road as calm as you please until their eyes met and he froze, his stunned expression matching her own. She blinked and he was gone. She turned to the south road and there he was again. Getting angry he ran loops around her, she spun and pinned him every time. "Oh, you're making me dizzy." she'd said after a few minutes and stopped chasing him around, then placed a hand to her temple to stop the swaying.

"Stop following me then." he yelled at her as he kept running in circles.

"Me? Following you! Sure, and every time I turn around there you are." she accused angrily.

"Then just leave." he demanded.

"Fine!" She arbitrarily picked the east road and walked at a brisk pace away from him, but the rest of the day, wherever she went she could sense him behind her. When she'd stopped for the night and found shelter in a nearby hayloft she broke the loaf of bread she'd pinched while it had been cooling in somebody's open window and laid half of it next to her in the hay.

"You might as well come and have a bite, you must be near to starved too." She took a bite out of her half of the bread and waited for him to decide whether or not to come out. "I know you're there hiding behind that watering can, you can't hide from me little fella." He stuck his head up over the handle and she smiled sweetly at him while nodding to the half loaf of bread beside her.

"It's yours if you want it."

Slowly he edged out from behind the can and made his way toward her. Keeping her in view from the corner of his eye he snatched up the bread and darted back across the barn and ate it in three huge gulps.

"My name's Cara, what's yours?"

"Ferris Bagley." he growled. "And lets be getting somethin' straight little miss" he jabbed a crooked, stubby finger at her, "I may be wee, but I ain't no *little fella*. I'm older than the number of hairs you got on that scrawny little head of yours, get it?"

She smiled and nodded, "Got it."

BACK IN THE FOREST she laughed and shook her head.

"What's so funny?" Ferris demanded from somewhere in the trees behind her.

"Oh I was just thinking how you've been traveling with me for almost four years now and it's a miracle that we've managed not to kill each other yet." She screwed the cap back on her canteen and tucked it in her pack.

"Humph! Don't know why I've stuck with you for so long anyway." he grumbled, peeking out from under a bush.

"You're free to leave any time."

"Sure and I'll be gone before you know it." he tossed back.

"Good. Let's get a move on." She rose to her feet and slung her backpack over her shoulders. She knew deep down that Ferris would never leave and deep down he knew that she would never want him to.

"I guess we'll carry on north for now." She pulled an elastic band off her slender wrist and pulled her mass of long chestnut hair into a tail on the back of her head, to keep it out of the way. Ever since that day she'd had all her hair cut off from the head mistress she refused to cut her hair

LURE

any shorter than the middle of her back, and she'd be damned if she let
some elf get close enough to tangle it up again.

They walked in silence, with Ferris following slightly behind her
which was the norm, except for sometimes when she decided to fill the
quiet with her own talking, but not this time. The sun was setting just
over the treetops while she walked every few steps with her eyes closed,
keeping a look out for any new folk that might be lurking around. She
was keeping an eye on a few that were still a couple of miles off, but so
far weren't heading towards them.

Suddenly she drew up short. She'd stopped so unexpectedly that
Ferris smacked right into the back of her legs.

"Eh!" he yelled and jumped back a near ten feet as if she'd scalded
him; Ferris couldn't abide human contact.

"What are you about, huh?" he fumed at her back.

"Shush." she hissed, "Thought I heard something." She angled her
head to the left, listening.

"I don't hear any…"

"There! You hear that?" she interrupted. "It's someone screaming."
She closed her eyes and concentrated harder on the hazes of light that
were near, "Ahh, a Far Darrig is about a mile that way… and he's not
alone." She pointed west, "must be a bog there."

"So what? If the Red Man has coaxed some gullible soul into his
lair there's nothing you can do about it, he's too far off." Ferris stated
matter-of-factly.

"Well we can try. C'mon Ferris, don't you want to drop in on your old
cousin, see what's up?" Cara cinched the straps of her backpack tighter
so it fit snugly against her spine.

"Just because we're of a related race doesn't mean we're family." he
snorted in disgust.

"Well I'm going, you gonna try to keep up with me?" she asked
him.

"I'll not be wasting me breath on some doomed soul." he sneered.

"Suit yourself." And Cara took off at a run as another scream sounded
through the darkening sky. She kept her mind's eye on the location of the
Red man ahead of her and watched as Ferris's yellow green haze waited
a few moments, then started after her.

She tore through the trees; long legs pumping, skipping over raised

47

roots and dodging low branches, her silver cross pendant she wore bounced slightly against her chest. It took her five minutes to reach the edge of the bog where she stopped to catch her breath. She saw that Ferris was still a ways behind her, his little legs can only move so fast, so she decided to go in without him.

She focused on the Red man's pink haze and was able to spot his small hut camouflaged in the bulrushes straight ahead. She stepped into the bog, her hiking boots sinking down into the soggy grass, the smell of rotting weeds and mildew turned her stomach but she kept walking, her footsteps squelching in the mud.

When she reached the small wooden cabin with its straw thatched roof she heard a woman crying inside, "No I won't do it, you can't make me." she sobbed. The sounds of a horrible, high pitched laugh bounced around the cabin like a pinball in a machine. Cara opened the door and ducked under the low eave and into a long rectangular room. She saw a young girl slumped on the stone floor, her face in her hands as she sobbed violently. Next to her was a fireplace with a large black pot hanging over a flickering fire, and in front of the girl was an old woman, her grey hair hung in ropes across her dead wrinkled face, a purple tongue protruded from her grey lips and her body stood slack, held up by an iron spike sticking up out of the floor, through her body, and the tip protruded from the top of her head.

It isn't real, it's just a vision, it's what he wants you to see. Cara repeated over and over in her head before the reality of the illusion took over. She stood straight and called out in a clear voice, "Na dean maggadh fum!" immediately the cruel laughing stopped. "Do not mock me!" she repeated in English just to be sure. She gazed around the room; the young girl was watching her, her cheeks stained from her tears, her short cap of almost burgundy red hair stood in spikes around her heart shaped face. Cara went to her and offered a hand to help her up.

"It's all right now, let's get you out of here." The young woman rose to her feet, seemingly floating as if she were weightless.

"Thank you." She sniffed.

Cara smiled and turned back for the door and was stopped by the stubby little man blocking their way.

"So you decided to show yourself after all?" she asked, keeping any hint of apprehension out of her voice.

"You've gone and spoiled my fun lass." The Red Man was only slightly taller than a leprechaun with a paunchy belly covered in grimy brown trousers and a red cape slung over his round shoulders. He glared at her, his eyes narrowed to slits.

"Yah, sorry about that." she spoke casually but tightened her grip on the girl's hand. "But you won't be fooling anyone else tonight with your twisted little games. Move aside before I kick you out of my way." she ordered and when he didn't move she advanced on him, tugging the girl behind her, until they were almost on top of him, then he vanished.

They rushed out the cabin door and made quick path back through the bog, the ground seemed to curdle and bubble as they walked; an echo of his hollow dead laugh chased them as they left.

"Just ignore him." Cara said as she picked up the pace and dragged the girl into the shelter of the trees.

She slung off her backpack and dug out the water canteen offering it to the girl, who timidly drank a few sips.

Cara sized her up as she drank. She looked pale, and not just from being scared but her complexion looked milky white and soft, like your hand would pass right through her should you touch her. She was willow thin and barely reached Cara's chin when she stood straight. The hair didn't seem quite right, she thought, and her eyes, something about those huge brown eyes that seemed to swallow her tiny face, looked familiar.

"Don't let what you saw in there worry you none, the Red Man is quite a rascal, gets his kicks out of playing pranks on unsuspecting people. It's all a bit of tomfoolery really." Cara tried to reassure her.

"Thank you." The young woman said as she handed Cara back the canteen, "For rescuing me from him." The air seemed to quiver around her like electricity as she looked back in the direction of the Red Man's hut. Fear, Cara realized.

"He wanted me to make a stew out of that horrible dead woman." she explained, her voice trembling. "Even if it wasn't real it was terrifying."

Cara replaced the water and slung on her pack. "I figure that makes us about even."

"What?"

"Nothing. So what is a trooping faerie like yourself doing out here, and alone at that?"

The girl's wide eyes turned from confused to alarmed, and she took a step back, "How... how do you know I am a faerie?"

"Same way I knew where to find the Red Man's hut and how I knew he wasn't alone, the same way I know there's a leprechaun making his way towards us from over there," she jerked her head to the east. "and he's taking his bloody time about it too." she muttered and smiled at the faerie. "Lets just say I can sense certain things, alright? Now, how about my question?"

The girl hesitated a moment, a battle of fear and trust played over her face. "My name is Feya. I left my troop when last the moon was full; my Mother has passed on to her next journey and I... I just... couldn't stay with them anymore." Her voice lowering to a whisper as if speaking the words would crush her. Cara couldn't blame her; a faerie that renounces their troop is condemned to death if they are ever found again.

"I see. So you're on the run as it is?" Cara confirmed, Feya nodded, her head bowed.

Finally Ferris burst through the brush and doubled over in two between them, wheezing shallow breaths and coughing, his beard tangled with briars.

"'Bout time you got here." Cara said. He snapped up straight, his chubby cheeks flushed from exertion and glowered at her as she smirked teasingly.

"Who's that?" he asked indicating the girl who looked about ready to bolt at any moment.

"That's Feya, she'll be coming with us." Both of them looked at her in astonishment. She started off walking north again and turned back to face them when no one moved. "Well? Come on then, we have to get a safe distance from the Red Man before he decides to come after me, we'll find a place to rest for tonight." And she disappeared in to the trees.

Seconds later, Feya was walking beside her; every movement was delicate and precise like she was gliding over a glassy lake. Cara looked down at her and she smiled back shyly. Cara closed her eyes for a moment to make sure Ferris was following, and chuckled softly at his grumblings that filtered up to them.

"I'm sorry about your Ma." Cara said as Feya walked beneath a branch that she had to duck under.

"It's alright, she's moved on now and probably better for it, but thank you."

Cara nodded and wondered about the reasons Feya had decided to leave her troop but didn't get the impression it was something she wanted to talk about.

"So… do you still play the pan pipes then?" she asked instead.

Chapter 7

"**W**HICH WAY TO BAGGAGE CHECK?" Spike asked as he looked around the crowded Dublin airport.

"You might want to try following that sign with those nifty little luggage pictures on it." Gannon said, his tone dripping with derision. He'd managed to look completely together, every strand of black hair slicked neatly into place over his narrow forehead, while the rest of the group looked like they'd been dragged through a knothole.

Spike shot daggers out of his eyes at him, "Oh yah? Why don't you try impaling your face on my fist a couple times?" he invited and held up his ham-sized fist in Gannon's arrogant face.

"Knock it off." Caleb ordered, as he rolled his neck trying to work out the kinks. He was tired and sore. In twenty-four hours he'd cajoled a major Pack Alpha, flown to New York, witnessed a possession, been thrown into a hostel alliance with two vampires, spent two hours in a stuffy library trying to track down any record of some seemingly arbitrary woman which had ended them up on an eleven hour flight to Ireland, and to top it all off like the cherry on a sundae, an ancient god had been released from hell to lead an army of demons in a war that would end the world. His strength and patience were wearing thin. He wanted to change. He wanted to hunt.

Seeing Caleb's energy deteriorate on the spot, Beckett stepped up between the quarreling wolf and vampire, "Alright, lets just find the bags and get out of here. We'll find a hotel and take a breather."

Oliver tugged Spike by the arm in the direction of the baggage carousel, and with a look from Beckett, Gannon followed.

"Thanks." Caleb said.

"Anytime." Beckett smiled reassuringly and headed off after the others.

THEY ALL STOOD SIDE by side watching the different bags go slowly in circles on the metal belt, eyes dazed like the methodical motion had lulled them into a watchful sleep, the sounds of flight announcements being called over the PA system, squeaky wheels on roll luggage and the animated tones of happy reunions all a buzzing din in the background.

"Hey Spike, isn't that yours?" Oliver noticed the army green duffle that had gone around twice was coming by again.

"Oh yah." Spike lurched out of his trance and hauled his enormous bag off the belt like it was filled with feathers. After the others had grabbed their bags they worked their way through the throng of people vying for a better position at the carousel. Oliver grabbed the back of his brother's coat and pulled him to a halt just before he led the group out through the sliding glass doors.

"Hey, doesn't sunlight, like, kill you guys?" he looked from Beckett to Gannon then to Caleb for confirmation.

"I think that's just a myth." Caleb replied.

"It is." Beckett affirmed, "Vampires lead a predominately nocturnal lifestyle and are rarely seen out in the day, because of course nighttime is more conducive to hunting for prey."

Spike and Oliver exchanged looks then carried on through the exit doors; obviously no one wanted to mention the fact that their 'prey' was usually that of the human variety.

They stepped out onto the sidewalk; the day was grey and drizzly but the air smelled fresh and almost sweet.

"Let's find a taxi and get to a hotel." Beckett looked around the busy lanes in front of the airport, cars coming and going."

"I'll ask this guy." Spike walked over to a small man in a black coat standing next to the entrance doors, "Excuse me, but I'm looking for a taxi."

The man's beady black eyes fluttered rapidly as he took in the enormous size of Spike but smiled a wide toothy grin, "Yes sir, I'll summon a cabby straight away." His Irish accent was so thick Spike didn't understand what he'd said until he saw the man raise his arm and signal for one of the black cars lined up on the street.

"Oh yah. Thanks." He walked back to the waiting group shaking his head, "Did you get a word that guy said?"

Caleb chuckled, "It'll be easier to understand their accent the longer we're here."

"I don't know about you but I don't plan on being here too long, we just gotta find this Cahill girl, get the answer on how to gank this Loke character, save the world and get back home." Spike stated as a tiny, black hackney cab pulled over to the curb in front of them.

"Somehow I don't think it'll be that easy." Beckett said as he picked up his suitcase.

"Yah, yah, story of our lives." Spike hauled his duffle over his shoulder; the inclusion of Caleb and Oliver in his statement didn't go unnoticed by Beckett.

"What is this supposed to be?" Spike asked when he saw the little car idling by the curb. He stood next to it and the roof barely reached his waist, "they expect all of us to fit into this tin can? My shoulders wouldn't even get through the door."

Caleb contemplated the car while scratching the day's growth of stubble on his chin that was halfway to a beard, "Well this just won't work." He looked around and noticed the Rent a Car desk through the glass doors back in the terminal. "How about an SUV?"

Twenty minutes later the group stood out in the Budget parking lot. "Well, it's not the Bat mobile but at least it's big." Beckett stated as he walked around to the back of the vehicle, popped the hatch and started tossing bags in the large trunk.

"I'll drive." Spike snatched the keys out of Beckett's hand as he shut the back door. He walked around the left side of the SUV and hopped in. "What the…?" He looked next to him at Beckett who sat at the steering wheel, an amused grin playing across his mouth.

"It's Ireland man, they drive on the right side of the car and the left side of the road."

"Crap!" Spike slammed his fist against the dashboard, "Hey, I forgot okay?" he glared over his shoulder at Caleb and his brother trying unsuccessfully to suppress their amusement, and Gannon sitting in the backseat looking insufferably smug. "Alright bloodsucker, just start driving."

Beckett started the engine.

CALEB SAT ON THE edge of one of the two double beds in the motel room they'd found about ten minutes from the airport. "Okay, we need to get all our ducks in a row here." He scrubbed his hands over his face wishing he could wipe the tiredness away.

"Ducks. I could go for some ducks, hey Ollie, they got ducks here in Ireland?" Spike spoke from his prone position on the floor, his hands behind his head.

"How the hell do I know?"

"Yes, they have ducks here but they're migratory birds, you won't find any at this time of year." Caleb examined the various occupants around the room and assessed the general mood. Everyone was on edge; he could almost hear the tension vibrating through the air like a plucked violin string. "We need to… regroup, rejuvenate." He met Beckett's eyes across the room. "We need to hunt."

Caleb watched the vampires for their reaction. Gannon was slouched in one of the upholstered chairs, staring idly out the window into the motel's parking lot. Beckett stood in the narrow doorway leading into the bathroom. In the short time they've been with the vampires Caleb had been studying them, to his analytical mind this was indeed a treat. For millennia the vampires and werewolves have lived completely separate from one another, so much so that a chance meeting between the two species was rare, and thus neither race knew much about the other. Of course there is legend dating back to the beginning of time, the stuff that's fueled such works as Bram Stoker's *Dracula*, and multiple urban myths, but all have been so convoluted by mankind that one cannot tell fact from fiction. A werewolf can always recognize a vampire, by their scent, their very presence sets the senses tingling; but it's not the same as sensing another of your own kind, like another werewolf, it's an instinct, it's danger.

Because of this fact, whenever either species has sensed one another near by, neither has ever tried to search out the other. The two have been enemies since the beginning of time, and nothing has changed. So such an alliance, however tentative, that these five have managed to form is virtually unheard of. Caleb couldn't help but watch and wonder about these two vampires.

Beckett turned his gaze to Caleb, his face contemplative, it hadn't taken Caleb long to figure out that Beckett was the authority. He wasn't sure how vampire hierarchy worked or what the exact relationship between the two was, but it was obvious that Beckett would take charge when necessary and Gannon would follow even if at times he seemed reluctant.

Caleb stood to face Beckett, who stood a little straighter when he did, "We hunt animals, exclusively. That isn't to say all werewolves do, human prey is… well, you see it isn't about the sustenance exactly, we can survive on normal food, it's the hunt itself that we crave, so humans are…" Caleb faltered in his attempt to explain,

"Humans are the ultimate prey to hunt." Beckett finished for him.

Caleb nodded, "Yes. They are, but neither Spike, Oliver, nor myself have ever killed a human, but that doesn't change the fact that we need to change forms and hunt regularly, and on a full moon we are forced to."

"Cal, are you sure you should be telling him all of this?" Oliver asked concerned, he'd come to stand behind Caleb. He didn't take his eyes off of Beckett's, they both knew that what Caleb had just shared was information that no werewolf would ever tell a vampire, and it was his way of offering a cord of alliance.

Beckett nodded, "You need to hunt. We need to eat." He flicked a glance at Gannon then back to Caleb, "Blood." he said, "We need blood to survive but it does not have to be human blood. I managed to pack a small supply of blood before we left, it isn't much but it should be enough for the two of us for a week or so." Beckett walked around the staring wolves and picked up his black suitcase and unzipped it on one of the beds. Inside were about two-dozen vacuum-sealed baggies of deep red blood.

"Don't worry," Beckett said, "they're deer blood."

Caleb let out a breath he hadn't realized he'd been holding. Beckett hid a smile by turning to the mini fridge in the console under the TV and started placing the small baggies inside.

"So, um, since you don't need human blood to survive…"? Caleb sighed in frustration at his sudden complete inability to express himself like a rational being.

Beckett stood and faced him squarely, "You have my personal

guarantee Alpha wolf, that no humans will be harmed by our hand as long as we are in alliance with each other."

Caleb smiled, vampire and werewolf shook hands, and both felt a new understanding had been reached.

That night, in a park just outside of the Dublin city limits, three wolves hunted in the dewy moonlight, while two vampires stood watch.

The next morning found the newly energized group at the National Archives building in the Dublin city center. Caleb delved right into the search, this was his area of expertise, reading, searching, discovering.

Beckett, he noticed, seemed daunted at first but there was a task at hand to be done and he noticeably squared his shoulders and set about leafing through the index, picking out records he felt would be useful, then sat down at a table across from Caleb and methodically began to read through it. Spike and Oliver took up sentry posts at the two doors leading in and out of the reading room and kept an ever vigilant watch, in the short time they'd had left in New York before their flight out Caleb hadn't been able to find out what packs territory, if any, Dublin belonged to. The possibility of entering into some foreign packs land unannounced had the twins on high alert. Gannon had taken up a corner table away from the group.

Caleb peered across the table and cleared his throat, Beckett looked up from the book he was reading, "I was just wondering how well you know Gannon." He flicked his eyes over to the vampire in the corner then back at the one seated across from him. "He just seems very, um… detached."

Beckett didn't say anything, just continued to stare at him. "I don't know anything about vampire politics, I mean I've heard that vampires tend to dwell in groups, um, nests I think they're called, and I thought, or wondered if you two were maybe from the same… I'm sorry I shouldn't have asked." Caleb stuttered to a halt and turned back to his book embarrassed, mentally kicking himself for prying where it was none of his business.

Beckett smiled and sat back in his chair, "Don't worry about it Alpha wolf, you won't offend me with your questions." Caleb looked up again and smiled sheepishly, "It's in my nature to enquire and I'm not an Alpha wolf, we're actually not a pack." Caleb explained.

Beckett sent a knowing look at the brothers guarding the entrance to the room, "Do they know that?"

Caleb followed his gaze, "I see your point."

Beckett sighed and looked over at Gannon, "I've known him a century or so; I was there at his birth."

"How are vampires born? If you don't mind me asking."

"A human is changed into a vampire by drinking the blood of a vampire. They then die and are reborn the following night."

"Really? So it isn't the bite of a vampire that changes you, as it is for us werewolves. Interesting." Caleb contemplated this new information for a moment. "I guess the makes sense, or else every person/thing you fed on would become a vampire, because your actual human body dies and you are reborn a new creation, a vampire."

"I suppose so." Beckett commented as he watched Caleb work through it in his mind. "You see, with werewolves, it is our bite that causes the change to happen in a human, that and the moon. And that's assuming the person doesn't die from the wound, the bite has to be non-fatal and has to survive until the first full moon when they will be forced to make their first change. So we are not killed and reborn, we are still humans only now with a slight advantage."

"Interesting theory." Beckett conceded, "One I would likely agree with but one which would also lead us down the long and winding path of, are vampires really alive or dead? Do we have souls? And frankly that's not a road I've been down and it has no end. So to answer your other question, Yes vampires do generally reside in groups. The word 'nest' is manmade. It implies that a bunch of vampires are holed up in some dark hovel somewhere, when in actuality they are bands, an assembly of vampires living in the same region." Beckett turned back to Caleb, "I assume it is somewhat similar to the werewolf packs, only they aren't families, there is less structure, and they don't hold to a territory. Vampire bands are migratory; rarely do they stay in one place for very long." Beckett leaned forward, placed his elbows on the table and rested his chin on his clasped fingers, his eyes trained on Caleb's, "If you're asking if Gannon and I are from the same band, that would be no, I haven't been a part of a band in a very long time. I've seen Gannon off and on over the years, crossed paths is more like it, but after the earthquake, as I was packing to head off to New York, Gannon showed up at my door."

"That didn't seem strange to you?" Caleb inquired.

Beckett shrugged, "maybe a little, I didn't think anyone knew where to find me and it's been decades since I've seen him, but you should never underestimate the wile of a vampire. Gannon said he was looking for answers and wanted to come with me. Since that was what I was in search of as well, who was I to say no." Beckett turned back to the record book in front of him and started reading again.

"But do you trust him?" Caleb asked.

Beckett smiled and looked up, "I feel the same way about prying into his life as you do about prying into mine, but he is still a young vamp, he is away from the protection of his band and vampires are not usually awake in the daytime; we're weaker in the day. So I am assuming any one of those things could account for his lackluster attitude. Also being in the presence of a couple of twitchy werewolves doesn't help matter's any." nodding his head to indicate Spike and Oliver hovering around the doorways. "But do I trust him?" Beckett paused, "As much as I trust anybody."

Caleb nodded at that and went back to his reading, he wanted to ask so much more but knew that his vampire history lesson was done for now. He couldn't help wondering though, how old Beckett was, if he considered a hundred year old vampire young?

FIVE HOURS OF SEARCHING turned up no information on Cara Cahill. Caleb slammed shut the big book in front of him, the loud slap resonated through the quiet reading room and had a few annoyed eyes turning their way. He rubbed his tired eyes and stretched back in the uncomfortable plastic chair, which bowed under the strain. "This is proving to be very futile; we've searched hundreds of birth records and found absolutely no mention of a Cara Cahill, or any Cahill."

Oliver left his post by the door and came over to stand beside Caleb; "Maybe you should take a break for lunch."

Caleb groaned and sat up, his body stiff from sitting and the lack of progress exhausting, "Maybe your right. What do you think?" he asked Beckett. "Head back to the motel, grab a bite?"

"Yah, this does seem like a lost cause."

They returned their records to the desk and started to leave when Gannon called over from his seat in the corner, "Wait, I think I've found something." Caleb excitedly rushed over, "What? Did you find her?"

"No mention of a Cara, but there are birth records of a James Cahill, born in Cork." Gannon flipped through a couple of pages, everyone was now leaned over the book trying to see. "James Cahill married Mary O'Gill and they had… two children, Ann and Margaret Cahill." Gannon looked up from the pages to everyone gathered around him and quickly stood up to let them have a better look and moved off a little ways.

Caleb sat down in Gannon's vacated seat and scanned the records, "This is excellent."

"Why? There's no mention of Cara, isn't she the one we're looking for?" Spike asked.

"Yes, but she could be related to this family, most likely is." Caleb stood up, new vigor in his movements, "either way it's the only lead we've got, good work Gannon." The vampire shrugged uncomfortably.

"Alright, well then, I'd say we get some food then go to the library, maybe there we can find some old newspaper articles on this family."

"Sounds like a plan." Spike clapped his beefy palms together, "So what are we doing, order in or take out?"

SINCE BECKETT AND GANNON didn't need to eat they headed straight to the library while the werewolves went to a nearby restaurant for lunch.

"It's nice not to have the wolf gang hanging over our shoulders for a few minutes, the Alpha seems alright but his guard dogs make me nervous." Gannon and Beckett were standing side by side staring at the neighboring microfiche screens.

"I don't think you need to worry about them," Beckett said as he flipped to another article, "as much as Caleb doesn't seem to want to admit he is their Alpha, he controls them and will continue to control whether he likes it or not."

"Yah, well this isn't what I signed up for." Gannon grumbled under his breath.

"What *did* you sign up for Gannon?" Beckett turned to the other vampire and noticed him visibly squirm before meeting his gaze.

"If the Twilight of the gods is going to wage war on earth, there's no one else I'd rather stand with than you." They stared at one another while Beckett contemplated this, and then turned back to his screen.

They worked on in silence until Caleb strode in a half hour later, "Any luck?" he asked.

"None yet. Just some vitals on James and his wife, I've got their obituaries printed off here and I found a small mention of his retirement from the local pharmaceutical plant in Cork," Beckett indicated a stack of papers on the desk beside him, "and we found the birth announcements for his two kids Ann and Margaret but nothing else. And no mention at all of a Cara anywhere."

Caleb was flipping through the printouts on the desk when something on the flashing microfiche caught his eye, "Wait!" he said, "Go back to that last article." Beckett stopped scanning and scrolled back to the previous page.

"*House Fire Kills Mother.*" Beckett read the title, "What about it?" Caleb held up a finger while he read through the article, then pointed halfway down the script, "Look here, *neighbors watched in silence as firefighters battled the blaze that engulfed the small two bedroom home. Once the flames died down enough for fire personnel to enter the residence it was too late, the remains of owner Margaret Cahill, 30, were discovered in her bed, authorities at first assumed she had been asleep when the fire started.*" Caleb read out loud from the article.

"Margaret Cahill, she's one of the daughters." Beckett said, "You caught her name at a glance while I was flipping through? Good eyes."

Caleb nodded absently, still peering at the screen, "*Upon hearing that Margaret was dead, neighbors immediately notified the rescue team that Margaret had two children, a seven year old daughter and an infant that lived with her.*" He continued reading farther down the article, "*while a thorough search of the house was being conducted the seven year old child arrived on the scene, it is believed she had spent the night at a friends house, but the girl being too distraught could not offer any information. The child was taken into social service custody and admitted to an orphanage in Dublin as there was no known relatives to claim her.*

Authorities later discovered that the fire was set from inside the bedroom and was most likely started by Margaret Cahill herself. The reason for this is still a mystery but as no remains of the infant were found in the house or anywhere in the neighboring area the police are calling it a kidnapping." Caleb stood up straight, "Daughters. She had two daughters."

"Mmm, I suppose one of them could be our girl." Beckett considered, "Let's hope it isn't the kidnapped one, as it appears she was never found and is more than likely dead, we'd need another medium to dig her up."

"So what do we do now?" Gannon asked.

"Well, I suppose we look into the girl who was taken to the orphanage, when was the article written?" Caleb asked.

"1990." Beckett said. "She was seven years old then, she'd be twenty-seven now."

Caleb strode over to the computer room across the library and booted up one of the sleeping machines.

"What's going on?" Oliver asked as he and Spike followed them in from the other room.

"We think we may have found her." Beckett offered as he stood off to the side of Caleb so Spike and Oliver could crowd in behind him.

"Blasted things are so slow," Caleb grumbled at the monitor, his finger anxiously thrumming on the mouse buttons. "Here Ollie, you work this thing, you're faster at it than I am." Caleb stood up and nudged Oliver down in front of the computer, "We're looking for orphanages in Dublin that were in operation back in 1990."

Oliver set to work searching the web, his fingers deftly flying over the keys. "There's none still in existence." Oliver stated after a few minutes.

"Darnit!" Caleb pounded his fist on the computer desk making the keyboard jump. He set to pacing, two steps of his long stride had him across the room before he had to turn and pace back again.

"There is only one children's home in operation in Dublin now and that one started in 2001." Oliver stated. He looked over to where Spike stood at the entrance, his bulk practically taking up the whole doorway. The brothers knew that when Caleb got agitated and focused on a problem he became less aware of his surroundings and thus became more vulnerable to threats, so they watched and protected.

"So a dead end?" Gannon asked.

Caleb stopped walking and sighed, "No, it's just an unfortunate set back. Beckett, where did that fire occur?"

"Castleblayney."

"Then that's where we go next."

Chapter 8

THE SUN WAS SHINING BRIGHTLY for a change; a gentle summer breeze wafted the scents of freshly bloomed roses and the sulphuric smell of gas up to Cara's nose. She leaned against her pale blue '95 Jetta, it'd seen better days; the paint was peeling off and had rusted through in many places. The passenger door wouldn't close unless you lifted when you pushed and jiggled the handle up and down a few times really fast, and the right side rear window never did roll up all the way, but it was her car, faithful, and she loved it.

Cara listened to the meter ticking as gas pumped into the gas tank. It was the type of day she should enjoy, one that should be spent at the cliffs near the ocean, relaxing, listening to the surf break against the rocks, and let the rejuvenating wind do it's work, but unfortunately she was nowhere near the shore and much too close to old memories. Just a few streets over was her old house, well, not exactly her old house, it had been burnt to the ground, but she assumed a new one had been built in its stead. She closed her eyes as a gust of wind lifted her mass of brown hair and tossed it around her face, on a sigh it died down and she opened them again. Looking over the rooftops she could see the trees of the forest she had escaped into one afternoon twenty years ago with a changeling strapped to her back. To the left of them was where her old house used to stand, every time she passed by Castleblaney she had to go into the town, it would be so easy to just by pass it completely and carry on, but she couldn't. She'd never been back to the house, however, not since the day the social worker had taken her away from it. Cara couldn't forget it, but she still couldn't face it.

The pump clicked and shut off indicating her tank was full, she replaced the pump handle and screwed the gas cap back on; the little round door to cover it had broken off years ago. Digging some bills out of her pant's pocket she bent over and peered in through the open driver's window, "You want anything?"

Feya sat in the passenger seat, her legs tucked up in a way Cara used to think was only possible for cats to manage, she looked up from the book she had open in her lap,

"No, I'm fine thanks."

Cara leaned her arms on the rolled down window and peered into the back, one of the seats were folded down, "Ferris? You want anything?"

"No!" came the curt reply from the dark hole leading into the trunk, Cara rolled her eyes and waited, "Skittles." Ferris conceded crossly.

Feya and Cara exchanged grins before she headed into the store to pay for the gas.

She slid back into the driver's seat, tossed the bag of skittles into the back and started the engine, the car stuttered a bit then roared to life, "Atta girl." Cara encouraged the car and patted it on the dashboard. She pulled up to the gas station exit and stopped, her eyes trained over the rooftops again.

"We can go by this time." Feya said quietly, "Is that what's been bothering you? Maybe if we go and see it, you can finally put it all behind you?"

Cara closed her eyes and checked for colours again, there were a few new ones she was keeping her eye on, for some reason they were making her nervous, obviously Feya had been able to tell.

"Nah, it's not that, I mean, it's not just that this time. That place is always going to haunt me," Cara said, shifting the car into gear and turned onto the road going the opposite direction. "I've just got this feeling that something is up, something big, you know?"

Feya shrugged, "I don't think I've felt anything different, but I'm not as in tune to things as you are."

"You know me," Cara tried for her best carefree smile, "It's probably just being in this blasted town again, what do you say we get outta here?" She turned the car left onto the R183; "We'll make Ballybay by nightfall."

"Off to Ballybay then." Feya went back to her book, Ferris munched on his skittles from inside the trunk, and Cara shifted the car up to speed.

"Good thing too. I could sure use a drink."

Just over the rooftops, in front of the house that had been built in place of Margaret Cahill's old one, stood a parked rental car. "The owners aren't home." Caleb announced as he walked back to the street from the house's front door where he'd just knocked with no answer.

"I guess we should talk to the neighbors, some of them might have lived here back then." Beckett suggested and scanned the neighboring houses.

"Oliver and Gannon, you two take that side of the street, Beckett and I will take this side, Spike, stay with the car." Caleb ordered.

"What?! Why do I have to stay with the car?" Spike demanded, crossing his arms in front of his mammoth chest, like an overgrown child about to pout.

"Spike, I need someone to keep watch." Caleb explained.

"Oh. Yah, sure, I got your backs." Spike puffed up as big as he could and swaggered around the front of the car, trying to look as menacing as possible.

"Good call." Beckett said under his breath when he and Caleb had walked a little distance away.

Caleb grinned, "Spike, God love him, isn't always the most diplomatic person. I figured it was best if he 'stood watch'."

Beckett laughed and turned down the front walk of the house next door to the old Cahill place. "There's two men around the side there, better let me do the talking." Before Caleb could interject Beckett strode up the front steps and around the side of the house. Two old men were sitting in rockers, a small table with a deck of cards dealt out between them.

"You're a bloody cheat O'Dell! These old eyes can't catch you in the act, but I knows it, you're swindling me somehow." one of the men accused the other as he slapped his hand of cards down on the table.

"Excuse us gentlemen." Beckett interrupted and both men looked up with a startle.

"Well, where did you come from?" O'Dell yelped as he clutched his chest, "Whistle when you're about to sneak up on a man that way."

"I'm terribly sorry." Beckett smiled and perched on the porch railing across from the two men. "You see my cousin and I are from America, we're here in Ireland doing some research on some old relatives."

"Ah, 'tis America is it?" The other man pulled a pair of glasses out of his shirt pocket and stuck them on his nose. "That one. He's from America too?" He asked of Caleb who was still standing by the corner of the house, not really sure what he was supposed to do.

Beckett grinned, obviously enjoying himself, "Yes, that's Caleb."

"Would you look at the size of him, you sure do grow 'em big over there." O' Dell turned to his friend, "Heaney, you see that one, look at the size of him!"

"Of course I can see him, I'm not blind." the one called Heaney exclaimed.

"Hello." Caleb gave a tentative wave and moved a bit closer to Beckett.

"Hmmm, so you're out lookin' for some long lost relatives are ye?" Heaney turned back to Beckett.

"Yes Sir. We were hoping to find somebody who was living around here back in the 90's."

"Well you're in luck lad, I'm Gil Heaney, this here is Seamus O'Dell, I've been living in this here house since 1962, so you'll want to talk to me."

"What are you on about?" O'Dell chided as he leaned forward in his rocker almost falling out of it, "You know there's been an O'Dell in these parts since before you was born."

Caleb came over and stood beside Beckett while the two men argued, "They seem to be getting riled, maybe we should…" Beckett interrupted Caleb with a barely perceptible shake of his head, the smile still on his face.

"Oh, well then I guess both of you would know of the family who owned the property next door here, Cahill was the name." Both men stopped talking and turned to Beckett.

"Ahh, grizzly business that was." Heaney said sadly, and both men crossed themselves in remembrance, fore head, chest, shoulder to shoulder.

"So, it's Miss. Margaret you're after wondering about." O'Dell sat back in his chair and folded his withered hands over his stomach. "Well the truth be told we didn't know much about her, kept to herself she did, but the girl… what was her name?"

"Cara." Caleb offered.

"That's it! Cara." Heaney slapped his hand on his thigh, "A sweeter child you never did see."

"Aye, 'twas that, a ray of sunshine she was, flittin' about happy as you please, always a kind word and cheery 'hello' she'd have for me."

"Aye, and me. And with such a weight on her tiny shoulders, her Mother, God rest her soul was hardly any use for the poor thing."

"Now that's the truth. Things weren't too bad until the baby came along… things just seemed to fall apart after that."

"Do you know whatever became of Cara?" Beckett asked.

"Taken to an orphanage in Dublin after the fire killed her Mother." O'Dell said.

"I heard she ran away though when she was a teenager, who knows what happened to the poor thing then." Heaney leaned closer to Beckett and whispered as if sharing a secret, "You know they said that Margaret started the fire herself?"

"You don't say?" Beckett feigned shock.

"Aye, they say her heart was broken after her baby was kidnapped."

"'Tis a cryin' shame." O'Dell mused.

"A cryin' shame." Heaney agreed.

Both men lapsed into silence, rocking in their chairs and thinking back. Beckett looked at Caleb and with a nod of his head indicated they should go since it seemed they weren't going to learn anymore here.

"Thank you gentlemen for your time."

"Not a problem son."

"Anytime."

Caleb and Beckett headed back to the car, "Well, we didn't really learn anymore than we already knew and are no closer to finding Cara Cahill." Beckett said. Caleb was silent as they came up to the car; Oliver and Gannon were already there.

"Any luck?" Beckett asked, they both shook their heads.

He leaned up against the car, "Well I'm getting pretty tired of these dead ends. What do you think Caleb?" Beckett asked, but Caleb was looking off into the distance, completely distracted. "Hey, what's up?" Beckett grabbed Caleb's arm to get his attention, Spike moved in closer and Beckett dropped his hand.

"Huh?" Caleb turned around to face the group again, "Sorry. What were you saying?"

Beckett eyes him curiously, "What were you thinking about?"

"I just… don't you feel it?" Caleb asked and looked back over his shoulder.

"Feel what?" Beckett asked, looking around at the others, who were now looking in the same direction too.

"A feeling, a pull, I can sense it."

"I can too." Spike said.

"Yah, it's weird, like something is calling me, that way." Oliver pointed eastward over the houses at the end of the street.

Beckett turned incredulous to Gannon, who said, "You seriously can't feel it?"

"You feel it too?" Beckett asked unbelieving. Gannon nodded and looked off to the East, "I don't know what it is, but I felt it the minute we got here."

Everyone else nodded their confirmation.

"Well, that's great, let's just forget about finding Cara and talk about our feelings." Beckett chided. "That'd be fine with me, the girl is starting to piss me off anyway, it shouldn't be this hard to find someone."

"Well let's just think about this logically for a moment." Caleb interjected.

"Please do." Beckett waved his hand for Caleb to continue and tugging at the collar of his leather jacket he leaned back against the door of the car.

"Maybe that has been our problem all along. What was it Lucille said back in New York?"

"Something about, if you look for her, you will find her." Gannon remembered.

"Yes. "Caleb said, "Maybe we've just been searching too hard, maybe it's time to listen and look with our instincts, with what our guts are telling us."

Beckett sighed and looked from one member of the group to another.

"Well what do we have to lose?" Caleb asked. "I'm not sure why you're not feeling it, but the rest of us definitely are sensing something, something telling us to go that way." Caleb again pointed east over the rooftops.

Beckett shook his head in defeat, "Well I guess since we're at another dead end, your guts are all that's left to go on." Beckett reached in through the passenger side window of the SUV and pulled a map out of the glove box. "East huh?" he opened the map and found their location with his finger and traced the direction. "Well east of here would be along the R183."

"And where would that take us?" Caleb asked.

"Doohamlet, Knocknamaddy and Ballybay."

Chapter 9

"Ah. Now there's my girl." Aiken's booming voice shouted over the fiddle music and stomping feet when Cara walked through the pub door. She smiled and rushed to hug the hearty bartender over the counter before taking up a stool. "How's she cuttin'?" he asked, and set about building her a pint.

"Grand altogether." Cara beamed at her dear old friend and relaxed into her seat a bit.

"It's been too long this time Cara." He scolded and set the glass of stout in front of her. His belly was rounder, she noticed, his hair a bit thinner, but his welcoming smile never brighter.

"I know, truly sorry I am for that Aiken. But, you know how it is."

He placed his large calloused hand over her small one on the polished bar top, his kind, blue eyes full of understanding, "That I do."

He was just what she needed, Cara decided, even more than the Guinness he'd poured. Whenever they came by this way Cara would always make a point to stop over in Ballybay just to visit Aiken's Drum; it's what he'd named his pub, he was Irish born, from a Scottish Mother, it was his homage to her and the old Scottish folk song she'd sung to him as a boy.

She glanced at the old wooden ladle he always kept nailed above the door that lead into the kitchen and asked, "How is your Mother?"

"Survivin' for the most part." He stood up and began wiping the bar with a cloth he kept tucked at his waist. "The cancer's back. The doctors don't hold out much hope for treatment battling it back much longer."

"I'm sorry." Cara said.

He nodded sadly, "I suppose you were by that way?"

73

"Filled up there, but…still couldn't go by the old street."

"'Tis only a stepmother would blame you for that, love." he spoke softly and with care before he strode off to help another patron.

Cara raised her glass in a salute to Aiken's Mother then let the dark velvet do its job.

As THE NIGHT WORE on, the music got louder, the dancing more lively, and Aiken watched as Cara became more and more uneasy. He stood at the far end of the bar, drying glasses as he watched her, slumped in her seat, nursing her beer. It seemed as if she had the weight of the very world on her shoulders. He remembered back when she was a child, they'd lived on the same street and he'd taken a shine to her right from the first time he'd seen her. It was hard not to, she'd come skipping up his front walk, a wilted bouquet of daisies clutched in her tiny hand which she so lovingly presented to his Mother, who was ailing even back then.

Aiken smiled softly at the memory, but it faded when he thought back to that day they'd taken her away after the fire. As he recalled he'd been parked down by the river, getting to know Miss. Alicia McKinnley a little better when the fire happened, and when he returned home that night, it'd been too late, Cara was gone.

He slapped a glass down on the shelf in frustration, what could he have done? He'd been a single, twenty-two year old dropout, working at any job that would have him, trying to scrimp up enough money to open his own pub; it's not like he could have taken care of a child.

He looked over at her and sighed, *I should have done something*. He'd known she was different, she'd trusted him, taken him into her confidence, her gift made her even more vulnerable and he could see that time had taken its toll on her.

"What's with Cara tonight?" Maureen asked Aiken as she pulled one of the clean glasses off the shelf behind him.

He jolted from his thoughts and smiled, "Oh, I guess she's just having one of *those* days, we've all had 'em."

"Don't I know it?" Maureen replied as she popped the top off a beer and started pouring it into a glass.

She was young too, maybe about Cara's age, her dark hair pulled back in a tail on top of her head. She worked a shift at the bar every night except on Wednesdays when Aiken forced her to take a night off.

Maureen was a single mother of two young boys, her man, if you can call him that, left her a year ago to fend for herself. He could see the dark circles under her eyes that she'd tried to lighten with make up and how lately she's had to wrap her apron strings an extra time around her already skinny frame from having lost weight. Why did all the women in his life have to bear such heavy burdens? He wondered sadly.

Maureen walked off to deliver the drinks, picking up a food order from the kitchen on her way by, when Aiken noticed the change, it was subtle but he saw it. Cara's shoulders stiffened as she sat up a little straighter on the bar stool, her eyes firmly shut.

Aiken walked over to her, leaned close so he could whisper but still be heard over the musician's lively jig, "What is it?"

"Can you see the man that just walked in?" She asked, her eyes still closed.

"Where?" Aiken kept his head bent close to hers and used his eyes to try to see around so he wouldn't be too obvious.

She shook her head slightly and opened her eyes, "He's over in the back corner, by the entrance to the jacks."

"I see a guy, his backs' to me though. He's wearin' a black leather jacket and got brown hair." Aiken said, straightening up, started to wipe the bar again with his ever ready cloth, "Is he different?"

"He is, but I'm not sure *what* he is. I've never come across a colour like this one's before, which means there's only a few things he can be…" Cara picked up her glass and downed the rest of her beer.

"You want me to get rid of him?" Aiken asked.

She smiled at his earnest and caring face, "Nah, don't you worry none about it, I'll show him the way out." She hopped off her stool and threw some bills down on the bar, and, Aiken noticed, a little extra for Maureen. "Thanks for the drink Aiken, hopefully it won't be as long 'til the next one. The best to your Mother, you hear?"

He watched her walk out the door and a few moments later, the man followed.

THE COOL AIR WAS refreshing. Cara sucked in a mouthful of the misty night air as she slowly walked to her parked car outside of Aiken's Drum. She knew the minute he'd stepped out of the bar and it was just the two of them. Or was it? She stopped just before she reached her car and he

75

stopped. Cara began rummaging through her bag as if looking for her keys, but with her eyes closed she was looking for something else. *Didn't come alone, did ya? How interesting.* Cara started walking again, and she noticed he did also.

She sauntered slowly, her car keys jangling merrily from her hand as if she didn't have a care in the world. The street was deserted. She could still hear the muffled sounds of music from the bar. She glanced up, the street was lit with lamps but because of the fog, visibility was low, she doubted she would be able to see her stalker if she turned around now, at least not with her actual eyes.

Still she didn't want a confrontation out in the open where anyone could just happen along and end up getting hurt. She could sense the others her new friend had brought along with him, a block down and two to her left, she knew they were together, and not local because she'd made them the minute they'd stepped off the plane in Dublin two days ago.

Cara picked up her pace a bit, tucked the keys back in her bag. *You came a long way to play fella. So alright then, let's play.* She took off at a run, her hair flying out behind her, she wished she had thought to tie it back, the extra length was a disadvantage at times like these, makes it easier for a pursuer to grab.

She increased her speed when suddenly she realized that she couldn't hear him running behind her, but with every blink of her eyes she could see him there, not trying to over take her, but keeping up with her. If her suspicions were right, Cara knew he could catch her if he wanted to, he could probably see her through the night mist, probably hear her heart pounding, blood pumping, smell... she stopped thinking, the fear was trying to force its way in and she couldn't let it.

It was annoying how her bag kept thumping against her hip as she ran so she yanked it off her shoulder and gripped it tightly as she dashed down a narrow alley between two stone buildings, she was heading right toward the others, might as well deal with them all at once she thought.

Her legs pumped harder as she felt her muscles begin to tire, ruthlessly demanding all the energy out of them she could. Darting around corners she wove her way through the back pathways in between the old shops until she came to a dead end, it was a small courtyard, only one way in and one way out.

She stood in the dark, all the shops were locked up tight for the night, there wasn't a light anywhere except for the moon up above. She closed her eyes, the others were there, but no one moved. Cara knew the only chance you have when dealing with supernaturals is to be unpredictable. She saw her chaser coming closer, once he turned that corner he'd be able to see her, so she picked the darkened doorway of one of the shops that wasn't occupied and ducked into the shadows just as the man in the leather jacket burst into the courtyard.

Cara could actually see him now; he was average height, maybe a few inches taller than her five-foot-eight. He had broad shoulders, and a narrow waist. He wore a white T-shirt under the leather jacket that was tucked it into a pair of slightly faded jeans that molded in all the places a pair of jeans should mold on a man. His hair was brown like Aiken had said, but now wind blown from running, and the dampness in the air had caused the ends to curl around the up-turned collar of his leather jacket.

Not that bad to look at, when a gals got the time, Cara thought, but she didn't have the time. Any second he or one of his buddies would realize where she was, when he turned his back to her she saw her split second of opportunity and took it. Stepping out of her hiding place she slid up behind him and shoved a gun firmly in the nape of his neck. Cara felt him tense and couldn't help a smug little smile, "I'm guessing this bullet won't kill you, but I wager it'll sting a bit."

Beckett grimaced, *stupid!* He chided himself. The little lady actually got the drop on him. He chuckled softly and raised his hands out to his sides.

"Slowly now, let's not have any sudden movements." She warned and pressed the gun harder against his neck. Beckett weighed his options, he could move fast, in one move he could have the gun away from her before she even realized what was happening, but the woman was smart and there was always a slim chance she'd get a shot off, he didn't exactly relish the idea of having his spinal cord shot out of his neck.

"Look, I'm not going to hurt you." Beckett raised his hands higher and turned his empty palms up so she could see he was unarmed.

"Uh-huh, it's not your hands I'm worried about."

"What?" He started to turn, thinking maybe he could catch her off guard, but the sound of the safety on her gun clicked loudly in his ear as she flicked it off stopped him.

"Let's keep those pretty fangs faced away from me, alright love?" She whispered in his ear, "and how about we have the rest of your little friends come out and join the fun?" she shouted into the shadows so everyone could hear.

Beckett looked in disbelief at the doorway where he knew Caleb was crouching. How did she know all this?

"Yes, that's right, I can see you all, let's all just come on out in the open and get to know one another shall we?"

Beckett dropped his hands to his side and shook his head, "Come on guys, the jig is up."

Caleb stepped out of his hiding place and into the moonlight, an abashed look on his face. Beckett listened closely to every steady beat of her heart, a woman completely in control, the slight clearing of her throat was her only sign of discomfort, which impressed him.

"Okay good, now the others." Gannon and Oliver stepped out from their places to the right. "And I see we have a stubborn one." she said, looking over Beckett's shoulder to the archway where Spike was hidden, the gun still steady on his neck. "Come here puppy, puppy, puppy." She wheedled with mock sweetness until Spike slunk into sight, his big hands fisted at his side

"What happened Beck?" Spike jeered at him, "The big old vampire getting the runaround from a human?" he shook his head and tsked, "What'll we hear of next?" Spike swaggered around to their right.

Vampire. So her assumptions had been right, Cara thought.

Beckett felt her watching the big werewolf and knew the moment her concentration slipped from the gun at his neck, just for a moment, but it was enough. Beckett swung in a flash of speed and leather, his left arm knocking the gun away from him, a simple twist of her wrist and the gun was free; tossing it to Spike he pinned her hands behind her back with his right hand, her body pressed tight against his as he bowed over her, her head tilting back so he could finally get a good look at her face.

An instant of fear flickered across her golden eyes, but he caught it before she could hide it. He liked them, the colour of wheat he thought, cat's eyes, cunning and beautiful. A narrow nose led down to a surprisingly full set of lips, naturally pink as he could see she wasn't wearing any make-up. His eyes traveled down the slender, white column of her neck and saw her pulse beating there. He watched the blood beat beneath her skin, mesmerizing, enticing. Beckett expected her fear, but when he saw and heard the rhythm of her heart slow he turned his gaze back to those liquid pools of gold she had for eyes. He could feel her tiny frame relax a bit against his; it was then he realized just how small she was which made him slacken his grip on her.

Beckett watched as she surveyed his face, her head tilted to the side, her nose crinkled and her eyes narrowed like she was trying to figure something out. He could feel the warmth of her breath on his face, the tips of her hair brushing against his hands clasped behind her back, when she said, barely above a whisper, "You have a heartbeat."

Beckett released her and stood up so fast, she stumbled trying to catch her balance. She'd surprised him twice that night, he didn't like the feeling, and turned his back on her he walked past Caleb and into the shadows, signaling for him to take the lead.

"UM, MAYBE WE SHOULD start off with introductions." Caleb offered, trying to keep a friendly tone to set her at ease, the poor woman looked like a deer caught in the head lights, she'd backed herself over to the corner of the courtyard near the entrance, probably so she could see the street and have an exit if she needed one, smart woman, Caleb smiled.

"I'm Caleb Colby, I'm a Professor at Duke University in the States, and this is Spike and Oliver." he gestured beside him to include the two brothers, who each nodded in turn. "You've, uh, met Beckett," Caleb acknowledged, "And this here is Gannon."

Cara straightened her stance and tried to look as tall and confident as she could, not an easy task when staring up at almost seven feet of werewolf. "I know how you found me, what I don't know is why you wanted to?"

"Well, maybe you could enlighten us, we aren't exactly sure how we found you." Caleb admitted, he took a step towards her but stopped when he saw her eyes dart towards the street then back again, he didn't want her to run.

"You've come a long way, from America you say?"

"That's right." Caleb answered.

"Mmm, I've been watching you since you got off the plane in Dublin, I saw you this afternoon in Castleblayney, didn't figure on you getting to me this fast, the only way to make it that fast is if you're actually looking for me." She looked at the group then back up at Caleb who seemed to be the one in authority right now, "So why don't we start there?"

"You are Cara Cahill, aren't you?" Caleb asked.

"I think you already know the answer to that." she replied.

Caleb nodded, "Yes, well, as you've already figured, we have been searching for you, but I really need to stress the point that no one here will in anyway harm you."

Cara looked at Beckett in the shadows behind him, his piercing green eyes, eerily the only part of him she could actually see in the moonlight, and didn't feel too confident about Caleb's assurance.

"In that case how about giving my gun back?" she asked Caleb holding her hand out and smiling sweetly.

Spike snorted, "Fat chance." and crossed his arms.

"Of course she can have her gun back." Caleb spoke firmly and Spike begrudgingly handed the weapon back to her.

Cara balanced the gun in her hands as if testing its weight, her eyes trained on the bulky werewolf as he moved in front of the tall one, very protective. She smiled as some things started to make sense and slipped her gun in the waistband behind her back.

"So," Cara leaned against the cold, stone wall at her back and crossed her arms, feeling more relaxed now that she had her gun safely back, "You were about to tell me why three werewolves and a couple a vampires were on the hunt for little ol' me."

Caleb was about to answer when suddenly there was a yell from the street, "Cara?" a man's voice boomed through the still night. Beckett leapt forward but Cara held him off with a shake of her head, "No, it's alright, it's just Aiken, the owner of the bar." *Dear, stupid Aiken*, Cara thought as he started walking towards her down the alley, his Daddy's old shotgun clutched in his hands.

"It's okay Aiken, I'm fine, just having a little chat with my new friends here." Cara tried for upbeat but was afraid it came off a little high pitched, so she smiled what she hoped was reassurance and started to lead Aiken back down the alley toward the street; just anywhere that wasn't near the shape shifters and bloodsuckers, but he pulled away from her and faced the group of supernaturals in the court yard, "Well I'm sure these gentlemen won't mind having your little chat with me and *my* friend here." He held up the shotgun.

Cara was starting to panic when at that moment a light from one of the apartments over the shops flicked on and they were bathed in light, "What the hell's goin' on down there?" a man's voice overhead shouted out of an open window.

"What is it?" a woman's voice called from farther in the apartment.

"There's someone down there, in the courtyard, probably them blasted kids again." the man replied. Cara looked up and could see the man's silhouette in the window frame, it was then Beckett stepped up to Aiken and held out his hand. "Hello Sir, I'm Beckett Graham." Aiken eyed him suspiciously but eventually shook his hand, Beckett smiled, "My colleagues and I do have some important business to discuss with Miss. Cahill, and as it seems we are disturbing the whole neighborhood, I was wondering if you might have a room in your establishment where we might be able to talk privately?"

Aiken looked from one member of the group to the next then back at Cara who nodded that it was okay.

"Ahh, alright, you can use the storeroom." Aiken offered.

"Thanks, Aiken." Cara picked up the bag she'd tossed in one of the doorways, made sure her keys were still in it then started back down the alley, the rest followed and they made their way back to the pub.

"Who *is* that down there?" the man in the apartment yelled down.

"Oh shut up Billy!" Aiken shouted up to him and lowered the gun to his side so his leg would hide it.

"Hey Aiken, that you? What are you about down there this time of night?"

"Nothin'. Thought I heard somethin', is all, go back to bed, ya eejit." And with that Aiken walked back to the street.

Chapter 10

AIKEN'S STOREROOM WAS A SMALL stone pantry off the back of the bar's kitchen, it was always cold and a bit damp, he'd lined the walls with metal shelving units which were full of canned goods, spices, ingredients, napkins, extra glasses and the like; the room was lit with one swinging light bulb strung from the ceiling.

Cara opened the door and walked in, pulling the chain on the light bulb fixture, it clicked on and cast a sickly yellow pall over the middle of the room leaving the corners shrouded in darkness.

"Cozy." Beckett remarked as he followed her in.

The rest of the group filed into the storeroom which now seemed a lot smaller. Cara stood with her back to the door leading into the kitchen, the vamps to her left, the werewolves to her right. It was obvious to her that this group, though traveling together, was still divided.

"Alright, start talking." Cara said and crossed her arms in front of her, "I want to know why vampires and a werewolf pack have joined forces and sought me out. I don't know much about vampires; I've never seen one before. As for your kind," she turned to face the werewolves, "I've come across them before, there's a small pack up North, I didn't stick around there too long though, territorial bunch, you understand." She cocked a hip and leaned against one of the metal shelves, which creaked as it shifted a bit. "It's safe to say I'm not an expert on either of your species, but I do know that you are natural born enemies... so what's going on?"

Caleb and Beckett looked at one another, "You take it Alpha wolf." Beckett offered, Caleb turned back to Cara and cleared his throat. "It all started three days ago... well I guess technically it started millions of years ago, but that's not really..."

"You're talking about the earthquake?" Cara interrupted.

"Yes, you felt it?" Caleb asked, getting back on track.

She nodded, "The news is stating it was felt everywhere, the scientists aren't very clear on what would cause such a wide spread tremor, they're saying there must be a fault line around the entire earth's core that has been building up energy for millennia. It's the only explanation."

"If only it were." Caleb said. "The quake wasn't caused by a release of energy built up around the earth's core, it was a release of demons from the underworld, the gates of hell have been locked up for thousands of years but now they've been opened on a raven's cry and all its prisoners are now here, on earth.

There was a moment of silence before Cara spoke, "You're kidding me right?"

She pressed the heels of her hands against her eyes and groaned in exasperation, "Oh, why is it always the crazy ones?" she spoke to no one in particular. Rubbing her hands down her face she sighed, "You've seriously come all this way to talk to me about demons?"

"You don't believe in demons?" Caleb asked.

"No." she answered.

"But you believe in werewolves and vampires."

"Never seen a demon." Cara retorted sharply.

"You said you'd never saw a vampire before, yet here we are." Beckett added. Which earned him a fuming stare.

"Unfortunately, it's much worse than just demons being released from hell. We believe that the earthquake and the raven's cry that followed was the first sign of Ragnarok, which means the end of the world." Caleb said, and Cara's eyes flicked back up to him.

"Ragnarok? Isn't that some old Scandinavian myth?" she asked.

"Yes, do you know it?"

"I don't remember all the details," she shook her head, "I read the story years ago, actually it was when I came across the wolf pack up in Northern Ireland. I was doing some research on them when I came across it. It had something to do with the werewolves conception doesn't it, how you came to be here on earth?"

"That's true, but the part we're currently concerned with is the end of that myth, the prophecy of the world ending."

Cara noticed a beer keg next to the shelf behind her; she took a seat on it and crossed her legs. "I don't remember much about the story. I know it has to do with the Norse gods and the valkyries."

"Look!" Spike interrupted. "We just need you to tell us how to kill the bastard and we'll be outta your hair." Spike stepped up from behind Caleb, his shoulders banging into the shelves as he tried to maneuver his girth around the cramped and crowded room.

"Kill who?" Cara asked and winced as a glass Spike had knocked off the shelf as he passed by tumbled off, but Oliver managed to snag it out of the air just before it smashed on the ground.

"Loke!" Spike yelled, getting frustrated, "That's why we're here. That crazy voodoo lady said you would have the answers we needed to kill this guy and stop him from destroying the world."

Cara squinted in confusion and looked to Caleb, "What is he talking about?"

Caleb placed a calming hand on Spike's shoulder, who sighed in exasperation and moved to go stare out the door again.

"Well it's kind of a long story," Caleb rubbed his forehead as he tried to think of a way to sum things up. "Alright, well… there are a few main characters in this story that we need to focus on." Cara noticed Caleb had changed to professor mode as if a switch had been flipped. "There's Odin and Freyja and Loke." Caleb counted them off on his fingers. "Now, as you may already know, Odin was the ruler of Asgard,"

"That's the gods kingdom right?" Cara asked.

"Correct, it is the Capital city of the god's realm." Caleb continued. "Freyja is the goddess of love, beauty, fertility, war and death, she presides over the afterlife field, or in other words, heaven. She is also the ruler of the valkyries. A Valkyrie is a minor female deity, they're purpose is to determine the victors on the battlefield, who lives, who dies, and out of the fallen men they would choose the most heroic and brave. They'd then fly on large black wolves with feathered wings to retrieve their souls and bring them back to Asgard. The souls were then divided up, half being sent to Valhalla which is a grand hall, where they will become einherjar, Odin's warriors whom he would train daily in preparation for Ragnarok, the other half are taken to the afterlife field."

"Yes, I remember that, the wolves and the einherjar," She looked at the vampires then the werewolves, "your ancestors." Beckett looked away and Caleb nodded confirmation.

"But the story goes on," he continued. "Loke is a trickster, a charlatan, a con man. He was born a jotunn, which in Norse is a giant, but he managed to fool the gods into making him a god. He enjoyed tricking people. He is very crafty, sneaky and malicious in his very nature. His pranks turned from annoying to dangerous and his ambitions more sinister. He worked his way up from disturbing people to destroying relationships, causing permanent injury or disfigurement, and eventually, death."

"Sounds like a tool." Cara commented. Oliver tried to disguise his laugh with a cough.

"Yes, that would be one word to describe him." Caleb smiled, "The prophesy states that the forces of evil and the underworld would rise up and march against the gods of Asgard, led of course by Loke. As we've seen, Odin knew this and was preparing for this by assembling and training his army of einherjar."

"So hold on, if Odin knew that Loke was going to be responsible for the end of the world why didn't he just kill him and be done with it?" Cara asked.

"Yah, that's sounds reasonable." Oliver added.

Caleb raked his hands through his hair and thought for a moment before speaking. "Well, it's my belief that Odin knew that Loke had a role to play in Ragnarok just as he knew he himself had a part to play. It was his destiny as well as Loke's and if there is one thing I've noticed through my whole life of classical studies it's that gods in general won't fight their destiny… only humans do."

Silence hung suspended for a moment, the light bulb swinging ever so slightly back and forth, causing the light to shift.

Caleb cleared his throat, "Anyway, the original foretelling of Ragnarok relates that at the end of the mighty battle the sun will be swallowed up, Midgard, which means 'Middle-land" or in other words, the Earth, will be set on fire and sink into the sea. But a new Earth will rise again and the remaining gods and two surviving humans will repopulate the world and they will all enjoy an existence of peace and harmony."

"Hmmm, are you sure that didn't already happen?" Cara asked. "I mean it sounds like you could be talking about Adam and Eve."

"True, but we are not living in a world of peace and harmony are we?" Caleb countered.

"Good point." Cara shifted her position on the keg and shrugged, "Okay, so what happened?"

"In that prophecy a lot of gods were destroyed but so was Loke, now he didn't like that so he started scheming and his plan essentially changed the entire fate of history." Caleb said.

"Well wait a minute, you just said gods didn't fight against their destiny." Cara leaned forward, her finger pointed at Caleb like she'd caught him up.

Caleb smiled, his eyes animated as he was enjoying the discussion, "Ah, but you forget that Loke is not really a god."

Cara sat back against the metal shelf again, her lips pursed, "Right, right, he was a giant.

"Loke was very resentful of the gods and he hates all of human kind, he wanted to destroy them all and when the world rises again after Ragnarok he would create his own new world with his wife Sigyn." Caleb paused, "Sigyn was a goddess and only one of Loke's wives but that is another story for another time." he explained before carrying on. "So, uh… where was I? Oh yes! You have to remember that Loke knew the prophecy for the end of the world, and his only chance to change the outcome was to change the players. Loke knew that Odin loved Freyja but she was married to a minor god named Ood. Loke goes to Odin at his hall in Valhalla and tells him that Freyja loved him in return but was bound to her husband. This of course was a lie to get Odin to kill Ood, which he did and broke Freyja's heart. Odin, seeing Loke's treachery imprisoned him in hell, bounding him to a stone underneath a serpent that drips venomous poison from his fangs. His wife Sigyn has spent eternity with him, holding a bowl over Loke's face, catching all the poison, but it's said that when the bowl is full she has to empty it and in the mean time the venom drips onto Loke and he writhes in pain causing the earth to shake."

Caleb stopped and realized this was turning into a lecture, "Unfortunately, the story doesn't end there, but to sum things up, a battle ensued in Asgard between Freyja's wolves and Odin's einherjar, gods fighting against gods, many of them died, including Odin and Freyja. What was left of the wolves and the einherjar retreated to Earth before Asgard crumbled and the world of the gods was completely destroyed. So of course with Loke imprisoned in hell and all the gods dead, it was believed that the threat of Ragnarok would not come to pass, until a few days ago that is."

"Oh that sounds great, the gods and the underworld choose Earth as their battleground and what? We're just collateral damage?"

"Essentially, except of course for the two lucky survivors." Caleb acknowledged.

"Okay, I get all that, but why do you think Loke is now free and why on earth does some voodoo lady assume I know how to kill him?" Cara inquired impatiently.

"Legend has it that Loke would break free from his prison in hell and the whole Earth would quake and a raven would cry and all the hosts of hell would escape with him. Because this myth dates back to ancient times, the details have been lost or forgotten to all but a few of us," Caleb spread his hands to indicate his group around the room, "When I heard the raven's cry, I knew what it meant and so did Beckett and Gannon, we met them three days ago in New York City when we both visited a friend of mine who happens to be a Medium." Caleb went on to explain what Lucille had told them and how they ended up in Ireland.

"…after we found the mention of your house burning down we went there to investigate but came up empty, that's when we all had this inexplicable feeling to come this way, something was pulling us here, and that's how we found you." Caleb ended.

"Except for you?" Cara stood up off the keg and moved toward Beckett. "You didn't feel the pull, nothing drawing you?" She looked up at him, her eyes narrowed, watching him closely.

"No." he replied.

She turned to Gannon, "You? Did you feel it?" she asked. He nodded curtly.

"Hmm, so it's not a vampire thing." She turned back to Beckett, "Wonder why not you?" She crinkled her nose, then turned to face Caleb. "Okay, that's a nice story." she told him, "But that's all it is, a story, it's a myth. I'm not sure you should be listening to crazy old ladies who send you off on wild goose chases across the ocean, but that's your problem

not mine, and I'm sorry to tell you I don't have any answers for you."
Cara held up her hands apologetically, "But it's been very nice meeting
you all but I really should go now." She walked around Caleb and started
heading for the door.

"But she said we would find you, that all we had to do was look for
you. How else can you explain us being drawn right to you?" Caleb
followed her.

She gave a wry laugh and looked up at him, "Trust me, the minute
you set foot in Ireland you'd have found me, as sure as death and taxes,
you'd have found me. If there really is a Loch Ness Monster out there,
someday she'll find me too." Cara said as she reached for the doorknob,
"Just another reason for me to keep my ass out of Scotland. That's all I'd
be needing, some bloody big sea monster chasing me through Inverness."
She mumbled more to herself and opened the door. "Don't worry though,
now that you know the pull is coming from me, you'll be able to fight
it off, at least for tonight, I'll be out of town first thing tomorrow, the
farther away I get the less you'll feel it."

Before Caleb could say anything to stop her from leaving, the door
to the kitchen opened and a young woman walked in, Cara turned to see
who it was. "Oh, hi Maureen, don't worry, we'll get out of your way, we
were just leaving."

Maureen had her back to them; she was shuffling things around on
one of the metal shelves but didn't say anything. Cara moved toward her,
"Maureen? Hey, you alright?"

Maureen still didn't respond. Cara was about to lift a hand to the
girls shoulder when she blinked and noticed something was wrong, there
was a black haze outlining the waitress' tiny frame, she started to pull
back but it was too late. Maureen whirled around, her eyes blazing blood
red, wielding a knife in her hand she lunged for Cara's throat.

Chapter 11

CARA SPUN QUICKLY, JUST IN time to have the paring knife Maureen had aimed at her neck miss its mark, but she wasn't fast enough. The blade sliced down her left shoulder cutting a bloody gash down her bicep. Gasping in pain Cara stumbled and was knocked off her feet when a heavy weight landed on her back. The air whooshed out of her chest as she landed hard on the stone floor. She was vaguely aware of people shouting around the room as she was flipped onto her back and stared up into Maureen's glowing red eyes. She was straddled over Cara's legs pinning her to the ground, one hand clamped around her neck the other holding the knife. Cara tried to cry out but the small hand around her neck tightened like a vise, cutting off her air. She grabbed the hand that was holding the knife as it started to slice down towards her throat, her hands were slippery from her own blood and Maureen was so strong. It didn't make any sense, the woman was barely eighty pounds soaking wet, but as hard has Cara fought, her legs kicking, trying to throw her off, it was no use. Just as she was about to lose consciousness something sent Maureen flying across the room where she smashed into one of the metal shelves. Cara gasped as she rolled onto her side trying to gulp air into her aching lungs, coughing she placed a hand to her neck where the skin was raw. She felt someone help her sit up and as she began to breathe steadily again she looked up into Oliver's concerned face, he was saying something but all she could hear was static. Shaking her head she looked across the room where Beckett and Spike had Maureen restrained against the wall. Suddenly the noise hit her like someone had turned up a stereo to full blast.

"What the hell is she?" Spike was yelling as he fought to keep hold of Maureen's right arm.

"She's awfully strong whatever she is." Beckett said and shoved her roughly against the wall to avoid being bitten.

Cara watched as Maureen thrashed and kicked against being restrained, her pretty face contorted in rage, her eyes wild and burning red as she snapped and snarled like a rabid dog.

"I think she's possessed." Caleb observed as he stood over them.

Cara looked back at Oliver who was trying to assess the damage done to her bleeding arm. "Are you okay?" he asked.

She was about to reply when she heard Spike say, "So how do we kill her?" He cursed as his arm brushed against the silver chain around Maureen's neck while he fought to hold her still. Beckett yanked the chain, which held a small oval locket, off her neck and tossed it across the room.

"No!" Cara yelled and jerked out of Oliver's grasp. All eyes turned on her as she shakily tried to get to her feet. "You can't kill her." she said and walked over beside Caleb, and looked at Maureen. It was hard to believe this was the same sweet girl who tirelessly served drinks in the bar, her whole tiny body vibrated while she practically snarled at them, white foam gathered in the corners of her mouth, and Cara could see that the werewolf and vampire were having a hard time restraining her, but she'd felt firsthand how strong she was.

"This is not Maureen, there is something in her, I can see it." Cara closed her eyes a second then looked imploringly up at Caleb. "There's a haze around her, it's not supernatural, it's dark, it's – it's otherworldly." She fumbled as she searched for the right word.

"Are you kidding me?" Spike shouted, "Look at her, she's evil."

"But you can't kill her, she has two boys at home who depend on her, she goes to church every Sunday, she's not evil, this isn't her, this isn't – normal!" Cara finished desperately.

"No, she's right." Caleb told Spike, "We shouldn't have to kill her, I'll try to exorcise her." Cara looked at Caleb hopefully as he pulled a gold medallion out of his blazer pocket. "You'll have to hold her down boys."

Cara stepped out of the way as Beckett and Spike moved Maureen to the ground, each pinning an arm and a leg to the floor while Caleb knelt beside her, the golden charm swinging from a chain in his hand.

"*Crux sacra sit mihi lux! Nunquam draco sit mihi dux. Vade retro Satana! Nunquam suade mihi vana! Sunt mala quae libas. Ipse venena bibas!*" Caleb's voice rang out loudly as he spoke in rhythmic Latin. They all watched as Maureen's body jerked in a spasm on the floor, her head tossing from side to side.

"You're hurting her!" Cara yelled and tried to lunge forward, but Oliver stopped her when Caleb held up a hand.

"Whatever you're going to do, do it fast!" Spike grunted as he and Beckett used all their combined force to keep Maureen still, but her wild flailing loosed her arm from Spike's grip and sent him crashing back into the door. Beckett managed to grab her other arm and pinned it behind her back, he wrapped his arm around her neck in a chokehold to keep her head from butting him and held her legs scissored between his. Beckett rolled on his back so Maureen was on top of him and facing Caleb, "Now!" he shouted and Caleb swung the medallion out over her body and shouted, "In the name of Jesus Christ, I command you out!"

Maureen's eyes flew open, her body stiffened and an unearthly cry screamed from her lips. A black mushroom cloud of smoke ripped from her body and radiated through the room like a big, black bomb of energy had exploded, the force knocking Beckett back into the mangled metal shelf behind him and everyone else fell to the ground, then it was gone.

Cara looked over to where Maureen's body lay unconscious on a bed of broken glass, Caleb was leaning over her, his large hand gently checking for a pulse at her neck. "She's alive, nothing seems to be broken." he said as he felt her limbs for fractures, "She'll probably have a bad concussion."

Cara slumped back against the wall, drew her knees up to her chest and rested her forehead on them. Her heart was racing and her breath was coming fast, she was going to hyperventilate if she let the panic take over, so she forced it down. Feeling someone sit next to her she looked up at Oliver again.

'We really ought to see how bad that arm is." He addressed her wounded arm, Cara smiled weakly and nodded. As Oliver started to pry the blood encrusted sleeve away from the cut, Cara looked over at Caleb who was still tending to Maureen, she met Beckett's serious eyes across the room when she felt a tingle of fear creep along her neck and she looked up and saw Gannon standing over her. He was staring at her arm, his eyes hungry, his mouth open; she watched his tongue play across his sharp canines. Cara cringed back against the wall as he took a step towards her, Oliver looked up but Beckett was already there. She hadn't seen him move but he was there, standing between her and Gannon. "Maybe you better go get some air." Beckett said to Gannon, who glowered, menacingly up at him. Oliver jumped to his feet and watched tensely the byplay between the two vampires. It looked at first like Gannon might challenge him but he gave in under Beckett's unflinching stare and backed down. Averting his eyes, Gannon strode over all the broken debris on the floor and out the door to the parking lot.

Beckett turned and knelt in front of Cara, "Let's take a look at that arm." But as he lifted a hand to her torn shirt she jerked it out of his reach.

"Get away from me." she glared at him and scooted farther away.

Beckett frowned slightly but stood up and nodded at Oliver to continue first aid before he walked back over to Caleb who was still trying to revive Maureen.

Oliver sat down beside her again, "I'm going to have to rip your shirt." he said, Cara shrugged.

"It's pretty much already ripped anyway." He grunted in agreement then tore the sleeve completely off. Cara pulled her tangled, bloody hair out of the way and twisted it around her right shoulder so she could see her cut more clearly. It was a jagged gash, messy but not too deep.

"Shouldn't need stitches," Oliver commented, "Just need some antiseptic and a bandage and you should be good to go."

Just then the door leading to the kitchen flew open and Aiken burst in, "What the hell is going…" He stopped short when he saw the state of the room. The music and sounds from the bar wafting in around him. Everyone watched in silence as he surveyed the scene. When he saw Maureen lying motionless on the floor and Cara bloody over in the corner with a werewolf bending over her, Aiken realized he forgot his gun. About to run from the room to go get it, Cara yelled after him, "Aiken! Wait! It's alright." Cara got to her feet, wincing at the pain in her arm, but went after him.

"Alright!?" Aiken yelled, his chest heaving heavily as his eyes wheeled about.

"Yes, it's alright." she spoke softly, laying a hand on his arm trying to calm him. Leading him back into the room, and over to where Maureen lay. "She's not dead, she's just unconscious."

Aiken felt for a pulse himself and seemed to settle a bit at finding one. He stood up again, "But what about your arm?" he asked, eyeing everyone in the room suspiciously.

"I don't have time to explain right now but I need you to do something for me." Cara explained, "I need you to take Maureen home and stay with her and her boys tonight until she is feeling better."

"But what happened?"

"Maureen will be able to tell you when she wakes up, I have a feeling she'll need to talk to someone about it. She's bound to be quite shook up."

Aiken watched Cara closely for a few moments, "Alright, but what about you?"

Cara smiled, "Don't worry about me, we need to get out of here and Maureen needs to rest."

"Okay, just let me clear everyone out of here and close up." Aiken walked back out through the kitchen, they listened while Aiken told all his patrons that he'd be closing early tonight; grumbling everyone left the bar. When the last car drove away Aiken came back in carrying a first aid kit. "Here." He said, handing the white case to Oliver. "Now, will one of you boys help me get her out to the car?" Aiken bent down to pick up Maureen's feet.

"Allow me, Sir." Caleb picked up Maureen like she was as light as a baby.

Aiken bristled a bit at Caleb's strength "Follow me, then." and he led Caleb out to his car.

When Caleb came back into the now destroyed pantry, Cara was sitting back on the beer keg, with Oliver just finishing up the bandage on her arm. She looked up and met his doleful expression with one of her own.

"Still don't believe in demons?" Caleb asked.

She sighed, and bent to pick up Maureen's locket out of the debris on the floor. "I'm afraid I'm starting to."

Chapter 12

CALEB DUCKED UNDER THE LOW doorway of the storeroom and out into the refreshing night air. The waxing moon shone brightly overhead, some of the fog had lifted from earlier that evening, and he could see the many stars speckling the black sky. Caleb took a deep breath, drinking in the moon's energy, in a few days it would be full, at its most powerful, and he and his werewolves would have to change. He could feel the lunar beams practically tugging on him, his muscles ached for the change, but he fought it off. Beckett came out and stepped up beside him, Caleb didn't take his gaze off of the moon, he knew who it was.

"Is there a problem I should know about?" Beckett asked, as they both stood side by side watching the sky. "I can sense some tension in you, Alpha Wolf."

Caleb laughed softly, "Problem? You mean other than being attacked by a demon possessed waitress and the world coming to an end?" He combed his hands through his hair, which was now long enough to rest on his shoulders. "This is the hardest phase of the lunar cycle, as the moon gets fuller, our wolf instincts get stronger. Back home we would change nearly every night at this time of the month and when the moon is full, we will have to change, it will force us to."

"By force, do you mean you have no control over when and where it will happen?"

Caleb nodded slowly, "It can happen at the most inopportune times, if you aren't prepared, our aggression grows and the fight or flight instinct is very strong and with our danger increasing, I'm bit concerned – I'm actually surprised neither of us changed tonight, when that happened?"

Caleb looked back through the open doorway to where Spike and Oliver were helping Cara tidy up the ransacked room as best they could.

Beckett placed a hand on Caleb's shoulder, "We'll deal with that when the time comes, like you said, you guys fought off the change tonight- but right now we have more pressing issues to deal with."

'You're right." Caleb agreed.

"For one thing, we need to find out what exactly is up with Miss Cahill in there." Beckett lowered his voice as he spoke. "I mean, she knew what we were and where you guys were hiding before, she lead me right to you down that alley."

"Yes, she does seem to have some sort of power." Caleb mused, "And how we were drawn right to her, it's like she drew us here with some sort of magic, actually I can still feel a pull right now."

Beckett watched her through the open door; she was crouched down holding a dustpan with her good arm while Oliver swept up broken glass, her long hair falling over her face. He didn't know what the others were talking about, he hadn't felt the pull that they had but he couldn't deny it was real. It had led them right to her, but the minute she'd held that gun to his neck and he'd turned and looked into those golden brown eyes, he'd felt something, something he wasn't completely comfortable with. Beckett cleared his throat and looked away, the street was empty, all the apartment windows dark, when he realized Gannon was nowhere to be found.

Spike and Oliver came out to join them, Cara locking the door to the storeroom as she shut it behind her and turned to face the group. "What was that golden charm you used on Maureen?" she asked Caleb.

"Charm? – oh, the medallion." Caleb drew the chain out of his pocket and handed it to her, "It's the medal of St. Benedict, the inscription on it is a prayer of exorcism, a prayer for strength in time of temptation, and a firm rejection of all that is evil." he explained as she studied the etchings on the gold disc. "I've never had an occasion to use it before."

Cara looked at him then handed the medal back to him, "Well, I'm very glad you had it and that it worked."

Caleb tucked the medal back in his pocket and surveyed the quiet neighborhood, "It seems we have a lot more to discuss, but I think we should find a more suitable place."

"I'm staying at a hotel for the night, it's just south of town by the river, there's always vacancy so you'll have no trouble getting a room if you wish." Cara closed her eyes a moment then headed to her car, "I assume you have a vehicle, you can follow me there." She unlocked her door and was about to get in when she turned to Beckett, "If you're worried about your *friend*, he's not too far from where we're headed, I assume he's walking it off." Caleb and Beckett exchanged baffled looks then she lowered herself into the drivers seat and started the ignition, "He'll find us when he's ready to come back." She shut the car door.

BECKETT DROVE THE WEREWOLVES in their rented SUV, following Cara's beat-up little Volkswagen through the sleeping town to an old historic building which had since been converted to a hotel. She led them around the big yellow house and parked in back. Beckett pulled the SUV next to her car and shut it off.

"Not bad." Beckett said. The hotel was backed onto a river, which was completely surrounded, by a dense forest.

"Uh-hmm, it seems promising." Caleb said as he got out of the car. "What's in these woods?" he asked Cara who was heading for a white door at the back of the building. The windows beside it were black from the absence of light within.

"There are two big estates on either side of the river, they have thousands of acres of wooded land. This immediate area is for the hotel guests, fishing is the main claim for this spot but I'd head North if you're looking not to be disturbed." She eyed him slyly over her shoulder, "and I'm assuming you don't want to be disturbed when hunting?"

Caleb cleared his throat, and smiled "No. That would be best."

"The Estate to the South has been restored to its original condition and they've thinned out a lot of the forest around it. Some of the family still lives there I believe. But the Northern Estate has pretty much been demolished due to forestry, but over the years they have replanted, and some of the original trees and what's left of some of the buildings are now being protected. I'd say there would be your safest bet." Cara unlocked the door with a key she had on a separate hook from that of her car keys and walked into the dark room.

Caleb followed her in but froze just inside the door. He grabbed Cara's arm and shoved her behind him, the force caught her off guard and she stumbled backwards, Beckett catching her before she fell out the door again. Caleb stood tensed, peering into the darkness. Spike and Oliver jumped up beside him, "What is it?" Spike asked, his muscles vibrating, ready for a fight.

"There's someone in here." Caleb stood straighter, his head skimming the ceiling.

"It's okay." Cara said, annoyingly brushing away Beckett's hand that still held her steady. She stepped in front of Caleb, "It's alright Feya, you can come out."

It seemed like she was speaking to the lamp on the bedside table, but Caleb watched as a figure materialized out of thin air; she was perched on the tiny table. He watched as she floated down to the floor and walked cautiously into the thin beam of moonlight splitting in through the open doorway. Her eyes were the first thing Caleb noticed, they were so big and round and brown, like the earth, he thought.

Standing at her full height she barely reached his chest, she was so small and slender and moved like a willow branch swaying in the breeze, her feet seemed to just skim the floor. Her milky white skin was smooth as porcelain and was such a shocking contrast to her spiky cap of dark cherry hair. He just stood staring down at her, like his feet were stuck there, but she was so beautiful he couldn't look away until he finally registered the expression in her eyes as she had to tilt her head way back to look at him. She looked terrified and was poised like a deer about to run from a predator. He suddenly stepped back and bumped into Oliver, "Sorry, sorry." He mumbled and tried to appear less intimidating somehow as her big eyes moved from him to the rest of the people in the room.

"Feya, this is Spike, Oliver, Caleb and Beckett." Cara introduced the group one by one, "Everyone, this is Feya, she's with me." Cara turned on the lamp by the bed and everyone blinked to adjust to the new light.

Feya moved close to Cara's side, "What are they?" she asked timidly.

"What are we?" Spike snorted indignantly, "What the hell is she? One minute she's not there the next she is."

Cara ignored his remark, "Well, those three are werewolves and that one is a vampire, there's another one out walking around the town, he got a bit hungry and needed to get some air." Cara guided Feya over to the one chair in the hotel room when her enormous eyes grew even bigger at the mention of vampires. "Here sit down, They won't hurt you."

"Wha – what do you mean hungry? Oh, he isn't hunting people is he?" Feya asked anxiously, wringing her hands together. Oddly enough she started flickering in and out of view, like she were an image from a projector that kept dropping out of focus.

"Hey, hey, just calm down." Cara knelt in front of her and grabbed her hands in her own. Feya took a deep breath and settled back into the chair.

"But why did you bring them here?" Feya asked.

Cara looked over at Caleb, "There is a lot we don't know about each other, maybe you'd better start over from the beginning…again."

"Oh my goodness, is your arm okay?" Feya asked once Caleb had finished retelling the whole story of how they ended up here and the previous events of the evening.

"Yes, it'll be fine in a day or two." Cara reassured her.

"And Maureen, she'll be fine?" Feya inquired of Caleb who had sat down on the floor at the foot of the bed so he could be at eye level.

"Yes, she should be alright, though she'll probably have some bad memories and a headache in the morning."

"So now it's your turn." Spike got up from where he had been reclining on the bed, "We've told you our story twice tonight, it's time for a little quid pro quo."

Cara was seated Indian style on top of the wooden desk next to Feya's chair, her bandaged arm tucked securely next to her body while she leaned back against the wall, "I suppose that's only fair." She picked up a pen off the desk with her good hand and started tapping it against her knee, "Feya is a Faerie." she began, looking around the room making sure she had everyone's attention, "we have many kinds of faeries in Ireland, she used to be part of the trooping faeries, that's a group of faeries who all band together, much like both of your species."

"You're no longer with your troop?" Caleb asked.

"No." Feya said sadly, her eyes downcast.

"I suppose your only knowledge of faeries comes from Disney movies but you must realize that is all ridiculous. Faeries are mischievous and are not without their malice. It's been said that the face of an angel hides the spirit of the devil. Do you want to continue?" Cara asked Feya.

"There isn't much to say." Feya tucked her knees up to her chest and rested her chin on them, like she was trying to hide as much of herself as possible. "My whole life my mother and I fought against the evil ways of the faeries, so many things they do and believe they don't even consider to be wrong, but stealing babies and their horrid tricks can cause a lot of harm and heartache for others. I just – couldn't be one of them anymore." Her voice faded off as a tear rolled down her pale cheek.

Cara leaned forward and stroked her back, "When Feya's mother died she ran away from her troop which was a very brave thing to do, she can never go back. Faeries are also bestowed with special gifts, as you have seen."

There was a moment of silence until Cara jumped off the desk and grabbed a bottle of water from the mini fridge on the other side of the bed, twisting off the top and took a drink. She met Beckett's gaze from where he stood looking out the window, "Still waiting for your friend? Don't worry, he's on his way back."

"How do you know that?" Beckett moved away from the window, letting the curtain he was holding slide back into place.

"Are you a faerie too?" Oliver asked.

"No," Cara laughed, "I've searched my whole life for an explanation of what I am, the only thing that you might be able to call me is a lure."

"A lure?" Caleb leapt to his feet excitedly, but stopped when he noticed Feya disappear in her chair.

"I'm sorry." she whispered apologetically when she came back into view, "it's an instinct."

"I'm sorry. I didn't mean to scare you." Caleb moved painfully slow, trying to make no sudden movements as he lowered himself down on the foot of the bed. Cara took another drink of water to hide her amused grin.

"You are a lure?" Caleb asked, turning towards her.

"Don't tell me you've heard of them?" she said.

"Once. I read an obscure myth in one of my studies, about what would happen if an incubus actually conceived with a human, it is believed that the offspring would have supernatural powers while still being a mortal.

LURE

It was thought that one of these powers might enable the child to draw other supernatural beings to them."

"We must have read the same study." Cara said, then went to stand behind Feya, placing the bottle of water on the desk. "It's the only source I've ever found mentioning it."

"So, you're a cambion?" Caleb asked, shocked.

"Hold on here, what are you guys talking about?" Spike interjected, "What is an incubus?"

"An incubus is a fallen angel who is believed to be able to take male form so he can sleep with human women." Caleb explained.

"Not a bad deal." Spike offered, flopping down on the bed again.

"Quite the contrary actually, it's supernatural rape. The sole reason an incubus has sex with a mortal woman is to hopefully produce offspring which are known as cambion." Caleb turned to face Cara again, "There has only been one cambion in history that was said to have actually lived, Merlin."

"Merlin? You mean the wizard from King Arthur?" Oliver asked.

Caleb nodded absently then continued, "usually after a woman has been raped by an incubus the physical pain and psychological damage it causes usually kills them, if by some rare chance the woman survives, the baby is usually pronounced dead at birth, due to the fact that cambion's are born without a pulse."

"But she has a pulse, I can hear it from here." Spike said, looking confused.

"Around the age of seven the child is supposed to start appearing completely normal except for whatever power being born of an incubus has left them with." Caleb finished while all eyes turned to Cara.

"So, your mother survived that attack?" Beckett asked.

"My mother fell in love with him," she replied, "she ran away from home when she found out she was pregnant, she gave birth to me in an apartment she had rented in Galway. She was alone, that's why you couldn't find any birth records for me, there were none." Cara moved back onto the desk, grimacing as she bumped her bad arm against the wall.

"My Mother spent her whole life waiting for him to return to her, it's what kept her going. She worked and raised me and eventually was able to buy that little house in Castleblayney. But I never saw him, she never told me his name, I don't even know if she knew it. Ultimately, he was responsible for her death, the strain of simply loving him was too much." She paused for a moment, "But as for my powers, I have no control over them. Every supernatural being within a two hundred mile radius will be drawn to me, the closer they are the stronger the pull becomes. I, on the other hand am able to sense supernatural beings, I call it my second sight. When I close my eyes I see flashes of color, mortals don't show up but every supernatural species has their own shade of colour, that's how I knew what you were and how I knew you were coming." She picked up the pen and started tapping again, "I keep a close eye on all the supers around, what type they are and where they're headed, as you can imagine most supernatural's enjoy their anonymity and don't want to be pulled to a mortal against their will, so we tend to keep moving. If we stayed in one place for too long, they'd all end up finding me."

Annoyed with the pen, Cara flicked it across the room into the corner and stood up, "So now that we've got the family histories out of the way I suggest we start focusing on the real problem here, but first I am going to take a shower to wash this blood out of my hair, and by the time I'm done Gannon will be back and we can come up with a game plan." Cara headed to the adjoining bathroom, "Feya, will you be alright?"

Feya glanced at Caleb then back at Cara, "I'll be fine."

Cara nodded slightly, "Just remember, I can see, even if I'm not here." She gave the general warning to everyone in the room, before walking into the bathroom.

Chapter 13

WHEN THE BATHROOM DOOR SHUT behind Cara and they heard the water start to run in the bathtub, Spike stretched like a giant cat waking from a nap then hopped to his feet, "Do you think they have room service here?"

"Doubtful." Oliver replied.

"I think this place is more of a bed and breakfast than a hotel." Caleb said rubbing his tired eyes as he heard Spike grind his teeth.

"There is an all night pizza place not too far away, we get them to deliver here sometimes." Feya said, her voice barely audible.

Spike grinned at her, "Do you know the number?"

"It's in the phone book." Feya opened the drawer in the desk beside her and placed the book on top next to the phone.

"Awesome! Thanks." Spike moved towards her when the door flew open and Gannon stepped in. Feya let out a tiny squeal of fright and vanished.

"What was that?" Spike asked, looking around the room.

She reappeared again in the corner behind Caleb, "I'm sorry, this whole situation is making me very jumpy." she apologized sheepishly.

Caleb turned and smiled down at her, "This is Gannon, he's the other vampire."

Gannon eyed Feya suspiciously, "What's with her?" he asked, but before anyone could answer Beckett grabbed his arm and pulled him back outside, slamming the door to the room behind him.

"Where did you go?" Beckett whispered angrily as he shoved Gannon against the side of the SUV.

"I got some air, like you suggested." Gannon snapped back and tried to walk around him, but Beckett gripped his shirt front and tugged him up to his face, "Don't lie to me," Beckett growled, "I can tell that you've fed."

Gannon tried to push him off but Beckett wouldn't budge, "Yah I fed alright, I smelled that blood from Cara's arm back at the pub and almost lost it, I'm not used to having to ration blood like this."

"You swore to me that you weren't feeding off of humans." Beckett accused, his eyes livid.

"I didn't! I swear I didn't! There's a lot of rabbits in these woods, I drained a few alright?" Gannon tugged at his shirt until Beckett let him go and he fell back onto the hood of the vehicle. "Beck, you're a bit tense, maybe *you* should eat something." Gannon brushed off his pants and smoothed his hair back in place.

"I'm sorry." Beckett apologized after a minute, "But I saw the way you were looking at Cara back there – "

"Look, it's not as easy for me, I haven't been off of humans as long as you have." Gannon interrupted.

"I know, but we need to work with these people, they need to be able to trust you, *I* need to be able to trust you."

"Alright, I promise to be more careful in the future." Gannon looked at the dent in the side of the car and laughed, "Do you think the wolf got insurance?"

Beckett grimaced, "I hope so."

"So, do we know anything more about Cara now? I could feel her drawing me to her the whole night, it was annoying, but I guess kind of a good thing in helping me find you guys again."

Beckett nodded then explained what Cara had told them earlier while Gannon had been gone.

Beckett lead the way back inside, Spike was at the desk ordering pizza over the telephone, Oliver lay on the bed with his eyes closed, and Caleb and Feya were talking quietly, she was seated back on the bedside table with Caleb facing her seated on the bed. As they shut the door to the outside behind them, the bathroom door opened and Cara walked out, a cloud of steam billowing out behind her. She'd changed clothes and had her mass of wet hair was pulled into a ponytail that trailed down her back.

"Well now that we're all back," she looked at Gannon and Beckett, "and all up to speed, I suggest we figure out what we're going to do."

"What I don't get, is why we were all brought together." Caleb said, twenty minutes later. They were all lounging around the room, ten large pizza boxes were scattered around the floor.

"What do you mean?" Oliver asked, tossing aside a piece of crust and reaching for another slice.

"Well, it's obvious that we were meant to all end up here, facing the end of the world together, why else would we have met up with Beckett and Gannon in New York? And why would Lucille have sent us all the way to Ireland to find Cara? Seems like a pretty big coincidence to me."

"Almost as if it were our destiny." Cara commented from her place in the desk chair, she'd eaten her fill of pizza and sat twisting the chair from side to side, her fingers tapping a steady beat on the desktop as she thought.

"Destiny seems to be a common theme we keep coming back to." Beckett stated from where he stood, leaning against the door, his arms crossed.

"Hmm, that's a good point, and if you look closely at all of our lives, we've all been dealt a hand by destiny and have fought against it to some extent." Caleb sat at the foot of the bed, he leaned forward, his elbows resting on his knees as he spoke, "I can't think of a more unlikely group, three werewolves who deserted their pack, two vampires who don't feed off of humans and live separate from any other band of their own kind. A faerie who's run away from her troop, and a mortal, with powers that have made it impossible for her to live a normal life and be constantly on the run."

"So what? We're all a bunch of rebel loners?" Spike asked, as he flipped the lids open on all the pizza boxes but kept coming up empty.

"Well I guess that's one way to think of it, it is what we all seem to have in common." Caleb contemplated. "I suppose it could be the strength in all of us coming together that just might tip the scales in our favor, all of our talents combining into one."

"Well I guess the main problem we're faced with now, is trying to figure out how to use each of our talents as you call them, and figure out just how exactly were going to stop Ragnarok from happening." Cara leaned forward in her seat, the springs in the chair creaking.

"Alright so what do we have in our arsenal?" Beckett thought out loud.

"Well you've got us." Oliver replied.

"That's right, your very own wolf gang." Spike piped up.

Beckett turned to the werewolves, "So what does that give us?"

"We're fast." Oliver said.

"Aside from being able to shape shift, all the attributes we have in wolf form also translate over to our human state. We have speed as Olly just mentioned, we can't move as fast as I saw you move Beckett, back at the bar, but we have incredible stamina, we're built for the long run." Caleb explained.

"We have good sense of smell and hearing, and the night vision is a huge bonus."

"Yah and I can bench press three times my bodyweight." Spike bragged and flexed his giant arms. Gannon rolled his eyes, "Oh what? You think you can take me bloodsucker?" Spike lunged to his feet, Gannon glared at him.

"Any day of the week."

"Gannon." Beckett warned.

"Spike, sit down." Caleb ordered, "You guys need to start getting along, we don't have time for this."

Spike backed down, "Sorry Cal."

"Okay." With a sigh Caleb pinched the bridge of his nose between his finger and thumb, "I guess that's pretty much it for our abilities."

"How do you guys change form? Does it take a long time?" Cara inquired.

"No, it takes only a few seconds, we usually do it on the run."

"Does it hurt?" Feya asked him.

He smiled over at her, his eyes soft, "Not anymore."

Seeing how the two were looking at each other Cara raised her eyebrows at Beckett, who shrugged and cleared his throat.

"So we know your strengths, what are your weaknesses?" Beckett asked.

"Weaknesses?" Caleb looked away from Feya.

"Yes, what can hurt you? What can – kill you?"

Cara pulled Maureen's locket out of her jeans pocket and held it in the palm of her hand, the silver felt cool against her skin, "Silver burns you." She stated.

"Yes, the mere touch of silver will burn us, if we are shot or stabbed with it, it will kill us, slowly and painfully, from the inside out." Caleb expounded on her comment. "We heal quickly, not immediately of course, but a regular bullet or knife wound that would be fatal to a human, we are able to recover from, unless it is silver."

Cara nodded slowly as she flipped open the locket and saw the two impish faces of Maureen's boys grinning up at her. Quickly snapping it shut again she slipped the necklace back into her pocket, it was too painful to even consider what it would have meant for those boys if things had turned out differently tonight, best not to think about it, she decided.

"Well, you all know what Feya and I have to offer, although I don't see how my abilities could be considered helpful." Cara said.

"Being able to sense other supernaturals and watch their movements could be a big benefit to us." Caleb added. "I was wondering, are you able to focus in on one being and make them come to you?"

"I've never tried it." she told him, "I can see all the supernatural beings within a two hundred mile radius, and I know that if I stay in one spot, they will all eventually get to me. But I have spent my whole life try to avoid that, I've never wanted to actually specifically draw one to me." With that she turned her attention to Beckett. He was watching her closely, those emerald green eyes piercing like he could see right into her mind. It made her uncomfortable, especially when she knew he was the only supernatural she had ever come across in her whole life that seemed immune to her lure.

"What do you guys bring to the table?" she asked him, meeting his unflinching gaze; she wouldn't give him the satisfaction of seeing how unnerved she was by him.

"We are fast, faster than the human eye can see, we are strong like the werewolves but weaker in the daylight."

"Why is that?" Feya asked, but she averted her eyes when Beckett turned to look at her. "If you don't mind me asking." she added meekly.

"In the myth that Caleb told you earlier, when Asgard was destroyed and the Valkyries wolves and Odin's einherjar warriors fled the kingdom to live on earth, the wolves became werewolves and the einherjar became vampires." Beckett explained.

"Really?" Feya's eyes brightened with curiosity as she thought about it. "Hmm, I guess that make sense, I should have made that connection earlier."

"As legend has it, while the einherjar lived in Valhalla they fed off of a saehrimnir, it was a giant beast, some believed it was a sea creature, some say it was more like a boar. But either way, every night the warriors would hunt the beast and feed off of it, draining its blood until death. Then every morning the beast would be brought back to life just so it could be hunted and killed again."

"Oh that sounds horrible, the poor creature." Feya cried.

"Since the einherjar were stronger when they fed, and they only hunted the beast at night, the vampires here on earth are weakened by the sunlight and strengthened at night when we would normally hunt."

"So that is why vampires need to drink blood? Because the ancient warriors used to feed off this beast's?" Cara asked and Beckett nodded. "Okay, so the sunlight won't kill you but it saps some of your strength, but what does kill you?"

Beckett started walking the room, his shoulders back, hands clasped behind him, "There are a lot of theories out there on vampires, a lot are not true but some of them are." Beckett turned to Cara, "For instance, holy water will not burn us but a crucifix will if it comes in contact with our skin. We do not need to be invited into a house to be able to cross the threshold, obviously, but we cannot step onto consecrated ground, like a church or a graveyard."

"Interesting." Caleb said, "so can you heal yourselves like we can?"

"Yes, we heal almost instantly, but we cannot regenerate, if you cut off our head we can't grow another back, but still that won't kill us."

"What? You mean you can live without a head?" Spike asked incredulously.

"True, we'd be pretty much useless, we wouldn't be able to feed, we'd eventually bleed out and our heart would stop beating, but we would still be alive."

"If you can call it that." Gannon interjected.

"So what does it? What would eventually kill you?" Oliver asked.

"The old classic wooden stake right through the heart." Beckett answered. Feya shivered and curled her legs up tighter around her.

"I've noticed that you don't have reflections when looking in a mirror or a window, but as Cara pointed out earlier, you do have a heartbeat."

"We drink the life essence of other creatures to keep our heart beating, a heart that pumps the blood of dead warriors through our veins." Beckett stopped in front of the window, peering out through the glass pane. The night sky had faded to a dark grey as morning drew closer. "We're cold to the touch and our visage cannot be reflected back to us because death, is the only thing keeping us alive."

Chapter 14

THE NEXT MORNING CARA WOKE with the sun. She stretched and turned her head to look out the windows, the sky was overcast, just the slight change in brightness had woken her. Groaning she sat up in bed, Feya was curled up in a tight little ball next to her, sound asleep, they'd only gotten to bed a few hours ago, but she knew she wouldn't be able to go back to sleep now so she swung her legs off the side of the bed and stood up.

Being as quiet as she could she walked over to her open suitcase next to the desk and rummaged through to find a clean pair of jeans and a white T-shirt, then tiptoed to the bathroom to get changed. She dropped her new clothes on the closed toilet seat and surveyed her self in the mirror. Her eyes were puffy from lack of sleep and her long hair was a matted mess around her shoulders. Sighing she splashed some cold water over her face then pulled off the over-sized, Def Leppard T-shirt she always slept in and tossed it on the floor. Picking up her hairbrush she'd left by the sink she started tugging it through her tangled hair, wincing as she struggled to comb out the knots.

Closing her eyes she took a survey of everyone around her, she saw Feya start to stir in the next room, and she could see the werewolves were still sleeping in their room a few doors down. She'd noticed throughout the night that the vampires didn't sleep.

Before they'd all retired to their own rooms last night they'd decided that they still didn't have enough information, and now that they'd all found each other, which they all agreed was important, they still had no idea where to go from here. Cara couldn't deny that something major was going down, and all the signs did point to that old Norse myth of

113

Ragnarok, but even with all she'd seen, and every unbelievable thing that she knows is out there, it was still a pretty hard pill to swallow. The end of the earth? Really? Why now? Why here? And did it involve her?

Setting her brush back down on the counter she noticed the scar running up her right forearm. Rubbing her thumb along the length of the raised skin she remembered her fight with a pooka that had attacked her while she slept behind a barn in Limerick when she was sixteen. He'd caught her off guard, she remembered, jolting awake when this dense weight of the tiny creature had landed on her, scratching and clawing at her. She'd lifted her arm to protect her face and the bastard's jagged claws raked the long scratch down her arm, giving her this scar.

Taking a step back from the counter she looked down at her feet, there were five identical puncture wound scars around each of her ankles, these ones she blamed on herself. It'd happened three years ago when Feya, Ferris, and she had spent the day at the shore in Dingle. She'd sat on the cliffs edge, her bare feet dangling over the side enjoying the wind, and the spray from the ocean misting her face. She could see the merrow's in the water down below, but not for a moment had she thought they'd manage to fly that great a distance out of the water, but that's just what they'd done. One managed to snag her ankles, digging its nails deep into her flesh it pulled her off the cliff and would have dragged her down to her death in the sea where she knew others were waiting, but she'd managed to grab hold of a rock and held on for dear life, frantically kicking trying to pry the determined sea creature off her legs.

Cara met her eyes in the bathroom mirror; turning sideways she lifted her hair off her bare back and looked at the many scars. She knew there were nine but counted them again, reliving every moment, every strike she'd felt while the faeries had flogged her back as a child in the stone circle, recalling as if it were yesterday instead of almost twenty years ago.

With one last look she let the curtain of dark hair fall back in place and started putting on her clean clothes. She didn't resent the scars that decaled her body, every mark was a constant warning for her to never let her guard down. She pulled her hair up into a messy mass on top of her head and secured it there with an elastic, then walked back into the main room.

"Good morning." Feya greeted her.

"Morning." Cara replied, "Get any sleep last night?"

"Some, it's hard to rest when everything is so... unsettled." Feya said.

"Mmm." Cara nodded absently as she dumped her old clothes in a pile back in her suitcase and shut the lid. "You better get ready and we'll get something to eat."

"Okay." Feya glided off the bed and started gathering her toiletries from the little canvas bag she kept all her belongings in.

"I'll go rouse the werewolves and see what Caleb has planned for today, since he seems to be running things right now."

"I think he said we needed to find out more about what we're up against." Feya commented.

"I guess that means research." Cara said as she pulled on her worn out Nike's and laced them up.

"Do you think that means we'll be heading somewhere else or staying here?" Feya asked, concern in her tone.

Cara paused at the door and looked at her friend over her shoulder, "I don't know, but don't worry about me, I've been keeping an eye on things." With that Cara opened the door and stepped outside. Shutting the door behind her she closed her eyes and leaned back against it. She didn't want Feya to be concerned but even if she tried to hide it, Feya knew from years of living together that she didn't like to stay in one place for more than a day or two; but she hadn't lied, Cara was keeping an eye on things, and by 'things', they both knew she meant the supernatural beings that were always closing in on her, closer every day.

Cara opened her eyes and stood up. Looking towards the parked cars she saw the back hatch of the SUV open, she knew he was there, she'd sensed him before she'd stepped out of the room. Taking the few steps down from the hotel she nearly missed stepping on some discarded pizza crusts that were left on the stairs. She walked over to the car and saw Beckett standing there, his back to her. He was dressed in dark blue jeans that hung off his narrow hips and nothing else. She couldn't help but admire his toned torso, pale skin and wavy brown hair, there was no sun shining but she could still pick up the reddish tints flecked through it. The air was chilly so she wrapped her arms around her middle and leaned her shoulder against the side of the car as she watched the muscles in his back flex as he tilted his head back and turned to face her, draining the last few red drops from the plastic baggy he was drinking from.

Cara swallowed a lump in her throat when she realized what he was drinking, she'd been too preoccupied appreciating his physique that she hadn't noticed what he was doing. His eyes met hers as he tossed the empty bag into the trunk of the SUV; she looked at all the empty baggies in the black valise and saw only three bags full of the thick red liquid.

"You only have three left." she stated, turning her attention back to him.

"Yes." his gaze hadn't moved from her face.

"Is this going to be a problem?" she asked.

"One we'll deal with when the time comes." He reached up to grab the back of the trunk door and slammed it shut.

"Well, when do you think the time will come?" she asked.

He took a step closer to her, "I can live on one a day."

"But there are two of you." He stood right in front of her, so close she tried to back up but bumped into the side of the car. "What?" she asked, her voice a whisper which annoyed her, she'd wanted to sound forceful to hide the fact she was completely unnerved.

"I make you nervous." Beckett said, his bare stomach barely an inch from hers, there was no heat coming from him but she could feel his breath making the wisps of hair that had fallen around her face flutter against her cheek.

Lowering her eyes to the pulse beating steadily in his neck she fingered the scar on her arm again, "It's only a fool who wouldn't be a little wary of you."

He laughed softly and looked to where her fingers played over the scar. Grasping her arm in his hand he lifted it, "What's this?" he asked.

"Just a reminder." she replied and jerked her arm out of his grasp. She watched his hand drop back down to his side when she noticed a red mark on his side, in the shape of a cross. Reaching out she lightly brushed her fingertips over it, his skin was cool and she felt him shiver slightly under her touch. "I see we all have our own little reminders." Beckett grabbed her around the back of her neck and tilted her face up to look at him, his eyes narrowed. " Old war wound?" she asked of the cross shaped scare.

"Self inflicted." He answered, his voice a low growl.

She felt his hard body press her back against the car and remembered being in this same position the night before, only this time she didn't want to push him away.

"What is it about you?" he asked, his voice rough and his eyes intensely searching her face for some kind of answer.

Cara felt her heart beat skip into overdrive, her knees felt rubbery and her head went light. She closed her eyes and still her eyes were filled with him. He lowered his mouth close to her ear, "What colour am I?" he whispered, his breath against her face sent tingles down her spine.

"Purple." she answered softly, tilting her head as she felt his lips run down the side of her neck. She didn't know what was going to happen, if he was going to kiss her or bite her but she didn't care, she just wanted the feeling of his cold touch on her. She ran her hands up his arms and gripped his shoulders, he felt like smooth stone, she felt herself sinking deliciously, he completely filled her senses.

Sighing she settled more intimately against him but jolted out of her haze when he quickly pulled away from her. She dropped her arms to her side and opened her eyes to see that he had practically jumped four feet away; he turned his back on her just as Caleb came around the side of the building.

"Good morning." Caleb called out with a small wave as he strode up to them. "Ready for some work today?"

"You mean more research?" Beckett asked and walked around to the other side of the car and opened the driver's side door.

"Knowledge is our only weapon right now." Caleb remarked and turned to Cara, his face concerned. "You okay?"

Startled by Caleb's voice she looked over at him, her eyes wide but she made herself smile. "I'm fine, fine." But she wasn't fine, what had she just about let happen? She stole a glance at Beckett through the car's tinted windows; he'd taken a black T-shirt out of his bag in the car and pulled it on over his head. She completely lost all sense of control around him, had it been some sort of vamp charm that had put her in a trance? He'd said he didn't feed off of humans and against all reasoning she trusted him, so she didn't believe he would have bit her. With an effort she calmed her breathing and slowed her heart rate, she knew both Caleb and Beckett would be able to hear how fast it was beating. But if it hadn't been some kind of vampire trick, then the other option was that she'd succumbed to him of her own will, and that idea was terrifying.

Caleb looked from one person to the other and got the feeling that he'd interrupted something, and not being sure to think of it he decided to let it drop.

"I've sent Spike and Oliver to pick up breakfast, they should be back soon." Caleb informed them and was about to say something else when he stopped suddenly and looked behind him at the door to their hotel room.

Cara was about to ask what was wrong when Beckett moved quickly in front of her, his arm outstretched to keep her back, she'd barely seen the flash of colour as he moved.

"There's something in the bushes." Beckett said.

Cara looked around him and closed her eyes, "Urgh, will you guys calm down! It's only Ferris."

"Who's Ferris?" Caleb asked, his eyes peering into the bushes trying to see something.

"Where's my breakfast?" came a grumpy voice from behind the green leaves of a small blackthorn bush that was growing up under the window.

Cara rolled her eyes, "He's a leprechaun, he's been with me since I ran away from the orphanage."

Beckett looked uncertain. "A leprechaun?"

"Wow! I can't see him." Caleb excitedly moved closer to the bush.

"You won't see him unless he wants you to." Cara told him, and then said to Ferris, "Have I ever forgotten to feed you? Honestly! I left you some pizza last night, which I can tell you ate from the crusts, breakfast is on the way, alright?"

They all stood staring at the bushes while they listened to Ferris complain in Gaelic which only Cara could understand, when suddenly the door to the room opened and Feya stuck her head out, "You guys better come see this." she called out to them before going back into the room, leaving the door open.

Caleb hurried up the stairs while Beckett and Cara followed, at the stairs Beckett stopped and motioned Cara forward, "After you." he invited.

She shook her head, "You first, I insist." she said, miming his movements. He stared at her for a moment then with a mock bow walked up the stairs and into the room. When Cara stepped up to follow, Ferris poked his head out of the thorny bush, "I saw that." He wheedled with a devilish grin.

"Shut up, or I won't give you breakfast." she retorted and shut the door behind her. "So what's going on?" she asked Feya.

"Look." Feya sat on the unmade bed, her legs tucked under her, and she pointed to the small television set.

Everyone looked at the news reporter on the screen.

"...temperatures are unusually low for this time of year, all across the country and with this weather system building over here to the West, we aren't expecting things to warm up any time soon. And now back to Debra at the news desk to recap our top news story this hour."

"Thanks, Jerry. The recent increase in crime rates seems to have taken the world by storm, in international news, every major city across the globe has experienced significant increases in random criminal activities. New York City reports a five percent increase in muggings, seven percent rise in rapes and assaults and a whopping ten percent increase in home burglaries, and all within the last forty-eight hours. Similar statistics are being seen in all major cities across every continent. Officials cannot find any connection to link the increase in crimes and are chalking it up to bad luck, crime rates are known to fluctuate and it seems we're in the midst of a world wide surge; but whatever the reason, police forces are certainly being kept busy.

And now on to local news, a man in Dublin was found in Marlay Park. He was unconscious and badly beaten when some joggers came across his body lying on the path early this morning. Paramedics were called and he was taken immediately to the hospital where he is being treated for numerous cuts and fractures. When he was able to talk to the police he stated that he and his friend were walking home from the pub around midnight last night when his friend turned on him with apparently no provocation, and beat him to within an inch of his life. The friend was brought in for questioning immediately after the victim's account and appeared to have no recollection of the attack or even knew that his friend was injured and in the hospital."

Spike and Oliver walked into the hotel room, both their arms full of brown take out bags and saw everyone fixated on the TV screen.

"What's happening?" Oliver asked.

The group watched another five minutes of accounts of random attacks all over Ireland before Caleb flicked off the TV and started pacing the room.

"Do you think this means something?" Cara asked.

Caleb raked his fingers through his hair, "It's further proof that the war is coming and coming soon." He snatched up the newspaper that Oliver had brought in started reading the headlines, "Brother stabs brother in local pub, eight year old girl beaten by group of peers, woman run down by neighbor, college student found murdered in alley..." Angrily he tossed the paper aside, "All these happened in the last twenty-four hours right here in Ballybay, not to mention the demon attack on Maureen."

Cara picked up the paper and leafed through it, Feya turned her tear stained face away. "All the attacks seem to be just injuring people, even internationally the increase seems to be crimes other than murder, but why was this college girl murdered here?"

"I don't know, maybe it was just a coincidence, maybe the murder would have happened anyway, but I think it's safe to say that the events of Ragnarok are underway and probably picking up speed." Caleb answered.

"Events, like the ones mentioned in that poem you read us back home?" Spike asked, "About brothers fighting..."

"Brothers will fight and kill each other, Sister's children will defile kinship. It is harsh in the world, Whoredom rife. Before the world goes headlong, no man will have mercy on another." Caleb stood at the window as he recited.

"What does that mean?" Cara asked when Caleb had finished.

He turned and faced the room, "It means things are about to get a lot worse."

Chapter 15

"SO ALL THESE CRIMES ARE related to Ragnarok?" Cara asked Caleb as he walked around the room, his head bowed making his hair, which she could swear had grown an inch since last night, fall across his face.

"It has to be, I'd like to do some more research to find out what exactly the signs of Ragnarok are. We know the earthquake is the first sign but there are others and they will get worse as the time for the final battle draws closer."

"How are you going to do this research?" Cara asked.

"Is there a library in town?" Caleb queried.

"The closest one is in Carrickmacross, it's about a half hour south of here and it's not exactly a world class library."

"Well it's our best shot for now. I brought all the books I had pertaining to the subject with me, but they are all in Scandinavian. I'll start going through them and translating anything I think may be important. Beckett, you have a laptop right?" Beckett nodded. "Check at the front desk of the hotel and see if they have some sort of internet, wireless would probably be too much to ask for. If they don't have any access maybe you could try around town at some coffee shops and try to search anything online." Caleb turned to Cara and Feya, "If you two wouldn't mind going to the library and seeing if there may be anything there we could find useful; I know it's a long shot but at this point we need to explore every option." He turned to Spike and Oliver, "You two will accompany the girls wherever they go. It's obvious that with the demon attack on Cara last night and the massive increase of crime just in this little county, I'd say we're making Loke nervous."

"You think he's watching us?" Feya asked alarmed.

"I think it's a safe bet to assume he'd be keeping an eye on us." Caleb said in all seriousness, "I'm not saying this to scare you," he said when he saw Feya start to flicker, "But we just need to take extra precautions for our safety."

Feya looked at Cara, then nodded and seemed to calm a bit.

"Alright let's get a move on." Cara stood up from the bed and headed for the door, "We're wasting time." She flung open the door, which Beckett had to catch before it swung and hit him, and stormed to her car. Feya smiled sheepishly as she walked past him as if to apologize for her friend's behavior, then joined Cara in her car.

Cara jiggled the key in the ignition a couple times before she found the sweet spot and got the engine roaring to life. Spike and Oliver jogged over before she left without them and managed to squeeze themselves in the back seat.

"Move over, man." Spike shouted angrily at his brother.

"I can't, the other half of the seat is folded down." Oliver yelled back.

"Leave the seat." Cara ordered and put the car into gear. Spike was about to argue when he noticed the tiny man climb through the opposite window in the back of the car and dart into the trunk through the folded down seat.

"What the…?!" Spike jolted against the side door making the whole car rock.

"Hey take it easy!" Cara yelled and backed away from the hotel.

"What was that?" Oliver asked.

"That's Ferris, he's my leprechaun." Cara replied.

"Your leprechaun?... Sure. Why not?" Oliver said casual and sat back against the faded car upholstery.

When they arrived at the Carrickmacross library, Oliver acted as security outside, while Spike followed Cara and Feya inside the small building and Ferris stayed in the trunk.

"They call this a library?" Spike jeered as they walked inside.

"I told Caleb this would pretty much be a waste of time." Cara said and smiled at the elderly woman at the checkout desk who sat stunned in her chair as she looked at the enormous size of Spike. Cara was sure the woman had never seen someone of quite that stature try to navigate their way between the tightly lined bookshelves. "But we might as well see what they've got."

"Hey lady, you got a computer in here?" Spike asked the librarian, who nodded slowly, her eyes wide behind her spectacles and pointed to the far corner of the room to a table with four out of date computers. "Great, that's where I'll be," he said to the girls as he headed in that direction, "if you need me, shout."

Cara rolled her eyes and Feya giggled, "doesn't he seem funny in here, like a bear trying to tiptoe around a maze of glass vases?"

Cara laughed, "It is quite a sight." The two scanned the headings at the end of each row of bookshelves; romance, horror, science fiction, biographies, when they came to a row with history on one side and academic textbooks on the other.

"I guess this section is our best shot, I'll take histories, you take textbooks." Cara instructed.

"Sure." Feya watched as Cara closed her eyes in a way she'd seen her do a hundred times. "Are we okay?"

"Some are getting closer than I'd like, but I'm sure we're fine." Cara tried to hide the distress she felt every time she closed her eyes and saw the colours closing in on her, but Feya could see through her disguise.

"If you run into any trouble, remember what Spike said, just shout."

Cara nodded and waved her friend off to the opposite side of the bookcase then started scanning the book titles for anything that even slightly related to Scandinavia. She spied two history books, one of Norway and one on Iceland, plucking them from the shelf she took them over to an old threadbare couch against the back wall of the room and started to flip through them.

After three hours of reading about every historic and geographic detail you could possibly want to know about the two countries, Cara shut the cover on the last page of Iceland and rubbed her tired eyes.

"Find anything useful?" Feya asked as she sat down on the couch next to Cara.

"Well, if you consider knowing that Iceland has a population of about

320,000 and a total area of 103,000 square kilometers then, yah, I found something useful."

"I didn't find anything either." Feya sat back dejected against the faded cushions on the couch.

"Although I did find one section in the Norway book that talked about these medieval wooden churches that were built all over the country, they have intricate wooden carvings on them which were believed to portray stories from their ancient mythology, but there are very few original works still standing." Cara stood and gathered up the two books, "But unfortunately that doesn't put us any farther ahead from where we are. Go get Spike and let's head back to the hotel."

Feya walked off to rouse Spike from where he sat dozing in front of a computer monitor while Cara went back to the bookshelves. She placed the books back where she'd found them then turned to leave when a fist caught her hard in the face sending her reeling back against the bookshelf then falling to her knees on the floor. Her vision blurred with white flashes behind her eyelids but she could still make out the pale blue outline.

"Crap you move fast!" she stated as she managed to sit back on her heels and look up at the furious faerie hovering over her. 'I just checked an hour ago and you were way over in Balgriggan."

"How dare you bring me here, mortal!" the faerie hissed at her.

Cara shook her head to try and clear the ringing in her ears, "Well I didn't do it on purpose." she replied. He raised is hand and struck her again, Cara felt the crack in her nose and fell onto her side.

"Hey!" she heard Spike's voice boom through the empty library as he started running towards them, but the faerie darted out of his reach and made to kick Cara in the stomach when she grabbed the iron nail she kept tucked in the side of her shoe. Twisting under his raised leg she jammed the large spike into back of his thigh. With a piercing shriek the faerie stumbled back grabbing at the iron spike that was sunk deep in his skin. Screaming in pain he yanked it out and tossed the bloody nail across the room then disappeared.

"Are you okay?" Feya knelt next to Cara who was still on her knees, her hands trying to staunch the flow of blood from her nose. "Is it broken?" Feya asked.

"Not this time." she answered.

"Here, use this." Feya handed Cara her cardigan she quickly slipped off.

"Thanks." Cara managed a weak smile and held the soft brown sweater to her nose and tilted her head back.

"Was it another demon?' Spike asked, looking around to be sure the man was nowhere around.

"What's going on?" Oliver asked, and he ran over to the group.

"How did you know something happened?" Cara asked as Spike helped her to her feet.

"We can sense when each other is in danger." Spike answered.

"Huh. Is that a twin thing or a werewolf thing?"

"Probably a little of both." Oliver replied. "So what was it?"

"Don't worry, it had nothing to do with demons or Loke or anything like that, just a random supernatural attack, it's nothing." Cara took the bloodstained shirt from her face and saw the bleeding had stopped, "Let's just get out of here."

Cara led the way past the shocked librarian and out the door to the car.

BECKETT WAS THE ONLY patron at the local internet café that had taken one of the sidewalk tables, a chilly wind was blowing from the west, having driven all other customers inside, making the balcony the ideal place for him, Beckett wanted to be alone.

He sat at a tiny wooden, round table, his black MacBook stood open next to a cup of now cold coffee. He'd been glad when Gannon had opted not to come with him in search of a wireless internet source; he'd lived in solitude for so long that being away from his compound in Northern Manitoba was very unsettling.

It would be ninety-one years this November that he'd made his retreat from the world; it was also at that time that he'd stopped feeding on humans. His brutal past had actually quenched that insatiable thirst for human blood that had fueled him his entire life until that day he'd stood over a field of slaughtered men, the needless butchering they wielded on each other, and for what? Land, politics, rights, ideals? Nothing really matters when faced with the immense loss of life, of loved ones; nothing is left standing when the bodies lay dead.

But Beckett had fought right beside them, firing his gun, killing as many uniforms as he could, it didn't matter what the colour of his uniform was, it only mattered that he shot the opposite. With the invention of guns, and flamethrowers, tanks and nerve gas, the fighting was no longer personal, or honorable, it had no purpose, it was all just a game, a sick and deadly game.

He'd rode many a mount into the frey, wielding a sword; he'd fought hand to hand and steel against steel when his horse was cut from underneath him. He'd fired flaming arrows at on-coming insurgents, battled back infantry with close range musket fire, feeding off the fallen, the blood of so many innocent mingled with his own on his hands.

He'd played on the losing team as many times as he'd been on the winning, it hadn't mattered what side he'd fought for, when it was all over, the treaties were signed, the dead were buried, the world moved forward and Beckett moved on to the next battle, until that final November day, he'd surveyed from a distance all the devastation he'd played a part in. Hundreds of dead and injured filled the trenches lined with machine guns, men blown apart from the introduction of armored tanks, the grey-green cloud of poisonous gas dissipating, leaving in its dust a slow and painful death when Beckett had finally felt the cold seep deep in his heart.

Sighing he sat back in his chair, it was all *her* fault, he decided peevishly as he fingered the full coffee cup on his table, he could still smell the last person who'd drank from that cup even though it's been cleaned. He could smell them everywhere; humans, but even the thought of feeding off of them turned his stomach, except for hers. Cara's scent was in his head like a cloud, hazy and dense, and no matter how hard he tried, he couldn't clear it. He could still feel her body pressed against his, he remembered the way she'd yielded against him, her skin soft, her pulse excited against his lips, he could have had her, right there pinned up against the car and, God help him, he'd almost did, her sweet scent was intoxicating but he'd retained enough sense to stop. Beckett knew that just one drop of her blood would be the death of them both because one taste would never be enough, but taking her life would surely kill him.

Angrily Beckett slammed his laptop closed and shoved it roughly into his leather case. It was useless for him to sit here and pretend to research when he couldn't get Cara out of his mind. It annoyed him beyond all reason, that a woman should affect him so, he'd seen millennia pass by and had never felt this way about a human being, a desire so strong to feed off of her, paired with a powerful need to protect her and he couldn't make sense of it. Sure she was beautiful, her tiny frame was sturdy but deceptively so for he'd felt the softness of her curves, her hair a silken lake he would gladly drown in, and her golden eyes haunted him every time he closed his own. She tried hard to appear strong and unyielding but he'd seen behind the armor she kept around herself and noticed the frailties beneath. Beckett remembered her instant look of fear when he'd disarmed her in the alley, her interest in discovering he wasn't affected by her lure and all the little nervous habits she didn't seem to realize she was doing.

Beckett placed some bills under the coffee cup on the table and carrying his briefcase started down the street to the parked SUV, still trying to reconcile the feelings Cara had stirring inside him. Unlocking the doors he tossed his bag in the back and climbed in the driver's side. With a groan he rested his forehead on the steering wheel, aside from the dark longing to feed off of her he also wrestled with a purely human desire to love her, to be with her. All his life humans had been his enemy, his opponents, his prey, his survival until he'd grown so disgusted with it all that he'd segregated himself away from everyone and every thing. To say Cara's powers didn't work on him would be a lie, because she was drawing him closer to her every second and he knew he wouldn't be able to fight it forever, he would have to have her, one way or another.

Sitting back in the driver's seat Beckett looked up into the gloomy grey sky and even though he knew his chances were slim he hoped somehow he wouldn't be doomed to an afterlife of hell because he was living it now.

Chapter 16

BACK IN HIS HOTEL ROOM Caleb sat hunched over the miniscule desk, not one inch of wood could be seen under the dozens of books and papers he had open and spread out on top of it. He'd spent the last four hours pouring over ancient texts, deciphering mythological prose and translating the difficult languages. He was going cross-eyed from the tiny print in some of the old books, Gannon had offered to help him with some of the translating since he could speak Norwegian and read a little bit of Icelandic, but they hadn't really gotten very far. Gannon had left an hour ago to give his eyes a rest and said he would pick up supper for everyone. Feeling discouraged, Caleb stood up and stretched out his kinked back muscles, his joints cracked pleasantly as he braced his hands on the ceiling and bent backwards. Dropping his hands to his side he rolled his stiff shoulders, his eyes lighting on the open pocket calendar above the desk, the tiny black circle on today's date told him that the moon would be full tonight.

"Well there's no use in fighting it," Caleb said to himself, "We'll have to change tonight." Running his hands through his hair he dislodged a pencil he'd stored behind his right ear, and gripping the ends of his hair he saw it'd grown long enough to tie in a ponytail. If he changed with it at this length he'd be one scruffy mess of a wolf. Dropping the pencil on top the cluttered desk Caleb went into the bathroom and started rummaging through Spike's shaving kit. He found the pair of clippers the brothers used the keep their hair buzzed short but decided against using it, the jarhead look was a bit too combative for his taste so he replaced the clippers and picked up a pair of scissors. Draping a towel over his shoulders Caleb spread his legs and bent his knees so he was low enough to see himself in the mirror and started snipping.

He was almost finished giving himself a haircut when he heard Beckett come into the room, he could feel his presence in the room, standing right behind him, but there was no reflection of him when he looked in the mirror. Caleb turned around and saw him leaning nonchalantly against the door jam.

"Finally got too long, eh?" Beckett grinned and nudged the pile of brown hair that littered the bathroom floor. "What's the matter? King of the canis lupus didn't want a mane?"

Caleb put down the scissors and tousled his now shorter hair, "Actually, the ancient valkyrie wolves all had fluffy black manes around their faces, but the long hair on a werewolf wouldn't give them a mane, it would just make their coat shaggier, which isn't a desirable condition considering the added length makes it more susceptible to tangles and getting things caught in it, such as briars and twigs and so forth."

Beckett laughed, "It was a joke, but good to know I guess."

"Oh… good one." Caleb smiled and shook out the towel around his neck, sending hair flying everywhere. "Hmm, guess I better try to sweep this up."

Caleb noticed Beckett staring back out into the room, his expression suddenly serious. "What is it?" he asked.

"I think the others are back from the library." Beckett answered.

"Oh, good. How about you go join them while I finish up here, then we can all compare notes."

Beckett nodded then left Caleb to his cleanup. Exiting the room he strode around the side of the hotel and saw the Jetta parked in front of the girl's room. As he was about to open the door he almost ran into Oliver who was coming out.

"Uh, sorry Beck." Oliver stepped around him and started to jog off.

"Hey, where are you going?' Becket called after him.

"To see if the front desk has an ice pack." Oliver shouted as he rounded the building.

Beckett entered the hotel room, Spike was hovering in front of Cara who was sitting in the desk chair, he was about to ask why Oliver needed an ice pack when looked at Cara's face; her left eye was red and nearly swollen shut and there was dried blood under her nose. Rushing over he shoved Spike out of the way and knelt down in front of her.

"What happened?" he demanded. Beckett felt the anger bubbling up inside his chest as Cara winced when she turned her eyes to look at him.

"Had a little fist fight." she said.

"Demon?"

"No, a faerie this time." she told him, "Just a random attack on your local lure."

Beckett saw the apprehension in her eyes as she gently removed her hands from the grasp he hadn't realized he'd had on them. Suddenly furious he rounded on Spike, "You were supposed to protect her!"

"I tried, the slimy bastard was too quick!"

"You tried?!" Beckett shouted.

"Stop it!" Feya yelled as she came in from the bathroom. Both men surprised, turned to face her as she walked in between them, a wet cloth in her hands. "There's nothing else Spike could have done." she explained to Beckett as she crouched next to Cara and cleaned the blood off her face, as gentle as a mother tending to an injured child. "Faerie's are hard to deal with, and we all have slightly different abilities so you never know exactly what you're up against, but Cara is better equipped than anyone with knowing how to fight them off and that's just what she did. It's just unfortunate that she was injured in the process." Standing up again, Feya went back to the bathroom to rinse the cloth, "But there is no use in blaming Spike for this, we were all caught off guard."

"Caught off guard? Aren't you supposed to be able to sense these things?" Beckett asked Cara, some of the anger died down but left him feeling frustrated.

"Yes, I did sense him." she retorted defensively, "I saw him when he was still miles away, I didn't think he'd be able to move so fast, but like Spike said, the slimy bastard was quick."

Oliver walked into the room before Beckett could press the issue further, he strode over to him and snatched the ice bag out of his hand, "Give me that." Beckett brought it over to Cara and placed it against her swollen eye.

"Give *me* that!" Cara said, feeling harassed, "I'll not be fussed over."

"You'll do as you're told." Beckett ordered, "and don't scowl, it'll hurt more." Cara glared at him out of her one good eye but gave up when she realized he was right.

"Alright, now you need to tell us where all the possible threats are that you can sense, so this doesn't happen again."

Cara stood up and faced Beckett, her hands defiantly on her hips, "Why, so someone can babysit me all day? This is my business, not yours."

Beckett appeared unmoved as he stared down at her belligerent face, "I'm about to make it my business, so deal with it." he stated firmly, all he wanted to do was hold her and comfort her but he knew she wouldn't let him and he wouldn't let himself; so instead he'd protect her, even if it killed him. Cara tossed up her hands in defeat and flopped back down in the chair, swiveling it away from Beckett and put the ice pack back on her eye.

CALEB ENTERED THE ROOM and noticed the tension immediately. Quickly assessing the situation he asked Beckett, who taken up a post behind the injured Cara, feet planted and shoulders back and had obviously taken control of the situation, what had happened.

After Beckett had explained, Caleb decided it was best not to mention to Cara that he agreed with Beckett's idea for keeping this sort of thing from happening again, and changed the subject.

"Did you guys have any luck at the library?"

"No, all we could find were some history books on Iceland and Norway, the only thing even remotely mentioning mythology was some old Viking churches that may have had stories carved on them." Cara told him.

"Stave churches," Caleb confirmed, "Yes, I've heard about them, there are very few originals left and no conclusive research has been done on the carvings. Beckett, did you find anything useful online?" Caleb asked, turning to Beckett.

"I came across a few websites that mentioned the myth's about Loke and Odin but didn't find any new information," Beckett replied, "I copy and pasted some stuff into a word document and saved it on my desktop if you want to look at any of it, I didn't have a printer so I couldn't run it off for you."

"Well Gannon and I didn't get too far." Caleb moved across the room and sat at the foot of the bed next to Feya.

"I like your hair." Feya smiled up at him.

"Thanks." Caleb blushed a little.

"Where is Gannon?" Beckett asked.

"He's gone to fetch supper for everyone. We've been translating my copy of the Prose Edda; it's an old Icelandic collection of verse retelling the Norse mythologies. It has three books and is quite long and it's slow going for us who have to translate it into English." Caleb told them apologetically.

"Hasn't anyone else ever translated it before?" Cara asked, setting aside the ice pack that was no longer cold.

"Yes they have, and I have copies of them, but I want to go through the original text and cross reference my translation with the others, I just want to be sure we don't miss anything important."

"So have you found anything yet?" Spike asked.

"We worked mainly on translating any part that mentioned Ragnarok and we did discover a few things. First we think that Loke's children will play a big part in the final fight."

"His children?" Feya asked.

"Yes, he had quite a few. Loke was born a giant but tricked his way into being a god, his first wife was Angrbooa, she was a giantess and she gave birth to a daughter, Hel who was half alive and half dead. Next was Fenrir, who took the form of a monstrous wolf and Jormungand who was a serpent known as the World Serpent. It's believed that Odin was afraid of Loke's strange children so he took Hel and placed her in the underworld which she presides over, then tossed Jormungand into the ocean here on Midgard, Earth, and he grew so large that through the oceans he can reach around the entire world and grasp his own tail."

"Oh, that's creepy." Feya whispered with a shiver. "What did he do with Fenrir?"

"Apparently they kept him in Asgard where they could keep an eye on him but that didn't work out too well. He grew so big and fierce that they needed a magic rope to bind him, they tied him to a boulder and drove the boulder one mile down into the earth and gagged him with a sword blade in his mouth. It's said when Ragnarok comes he will break free and join his father and siblings in the battle. I don't know if this means he broke free when his father did or if he is still there until the actual fight." Caleb explained, "But Loke had another wife, Sigyn, you may remember, she was the one who held the bowl over his face to catch the venom from dripping on him while he was imprisoned."

"So what do they all have to do with the end of the world?" Beckett asked.

"Well the original prophesy claimed that once Loke broke free of his prison he would start collecting his army."

"Who is Loke's army?" Spike inquired and lowered himself to a seated position on the floor.

"The Prose states that the gods of Asgard would march to meet the Jotunn, or giants, Loke's children, Hel, Fenrir and the serpent as well as Loke himself."

"But that wouldn't be much of an army, Loke and his three kids." Oliver considered.

"Don't forget the giants." Caleb reminded.

"But wouldn't the giants have died when Asgard was destroyed?" Feya asked.

"Not necessarily, the giants lived in their own land separate from the gods in Asgard and from the humans here on earth, it was called Jotunheim and for all we know and I think we should assume, that it does still exist and could be a big threat to us."

EVENING CAME AND SO did Gannon with another batch of takeout food. The group settled around the room again, each adding their ideas and thoughts to the discussion.

"It makes sense to me that if there are giants out there somewhere, Loke will recruit them, he used to be one of them after all." Beckett reasoned, from where he leaned against the desk, not having left Cara's side all evening.

"As for Loke's children, it's my belief that since his daughter Hel runs the underworld, she would be responsible for rounding up all the demons that escaped with Loke which means he'd have them under his control too."

"Since we've had a demon attack aimed directly at us, I'd say that sounds likely." Cara agreed. "But what about the serpent and the wolf?"

"I don't think the serpent would pose much of a threat, he's confined to the oceans but Fenrir the wolf does seem formidable." Beckett said as he considered every angle.

"Well I'll say what no one here wants to, we're all thinking that if Hel is going to bring the demons and Loke the giants, then it's logical to assume that Fenrir will somehow lead an army of werewolves." Caleb waited for comments but was met with silence and concerned looks from Spike and Oliver.

"Okay, let's assume that's true for a second," Beckett said, "how would he be able to get to every werewolf in the world and convince them to join forces with him?"

"It does seem unrealistic, but we shouldn't dismiss any potential threat." Caleb reasoned, "We've got three werewolves here on our team, if Loke tries anything with the wolves, we will know." Caleb said, trying to put everyone's unspoken fears to rest, at least for the time being.

"I translated a small part of the prose earlier this morning that talked about the signs of Ragnarok coming." Gannon said. Everyone turned his way with surprise showing on their faces, Gannon was actually adding something to the conversation.

"Wow, it speaks!" Spike exclaimed rudely.

Ignoring Spike's comment Caleb urged Gannon to continue.

"It read that the world would experience a fimbul winter…" Gannon said.

"What does that mean?" Beckett interrupted.

"From what I could gather, a fimbul winter is three consecutive months of winter." Gannon explained.

"What else did it say we should expect?" Caleb asked.

"It said that during the winters the sun will grow dim and be extinguished completely as the battle is about to start. Evil forces will be released, which we've already discovered and wars will rage among the humans."

"Complete chaos will rule the world before the final fight and there will be no army of gods coming to fight it for us." Caleb concluded and looked through the open window, the moon was full, it was time to hunt.

Chapter 17

CARA PACED ANXIOUSLY AROUND THE hotel room, everyone had left, the werewolves to prepare for their hunt and Gannon would stand watch at the edge of the woods, the hotel was pretty secluded and the only other guests had left early that morning, so it was unlikely that anyone would be wandering in the woods, but it was better to be safe than sorry.

Cara stopped in front of the window and gazed up at the night sky, the giant, white orb of the moon shining like a spotlight against a dark stage.

"Do you think the woods will be empty?" Cara asked Feya who sat watching her from the desk chair.

"It should be at this time of night, it's nearly ten o' clock, anyone from the town who'd been at the lake for fishing would be long gone by now." Feya replied. She could tell Cara was worried by the way she kept wringing her hands together.

Cara looked down and saw Beckett and Gannon huddled around the back end of the SUV. "They're almost out of blood." Cara stated flatly. "I saw this morning they only had three bags left."

"We can't worry about that now." Feya saw the moment of calm settled over Cara's countenance and braced for the storm; she'd seen it before, Cara's breaking point.

"Well someone has to worry about it!" Cara whirled from the window, Feya stood up.

"It'll be alright, Cara." Feya spoke soothingly.

"How?! How on earth is it going to be alright?" Cara paced frantically, her knuckles turning white from her hands clenching and unclenching.

"We're stuck in this place on a full moon with three werewolves who might go berserk if they don't change forms, two vampires who only have a day's supply of blood left before they'll be looking for other sources… live sources. And that isn't even mentioning the fact we've got a crazy Norse god after us and the fate of the world resting on our shoulders!"

Beckett came back into the room, "The guys are off for their hunt, Gannon is standing watch… what's going on?" he asked when he saw how agitated Cara was.

"She's having a panic attack." Feya informed him, "Cara, here…just stop." Feya grabbed Cara's shoulders and stopped her traipsing about the room.

"They're getting closer Feya, I can feel them." Cara cried and clutched her friend's hands, "You know what that means, you know what they will do to me." On a harsh whisper Cara finally broke and the tears started down her cheeks.

Beckett stood by watching, feeling helpless and not sure what he should do.

"I know we need to move on and we will, I promise." Feya led Cara's trembling form over to the bed and helped her lay down. "I'll tell Caleb as soon as he gets back that we need to move to a new location, and we'll go right away."

"You promise?" Cara sniffled back the tears and lay down.

"I promise, you just need to relax." Feya placed a gentle touch on Cara's hands and eased the tension there.

Cara turned her head and saw Beckett hovering near the foot of the bed, "Make him go away." Cara said to Feya.

"I'm not going anywhere." Beckett's tone was firm.

Feya looked at him, then back at Cara, "He's here to protect us, so you just stop worrying and go to sleep." Feya smoothed her long hair out on the pillow and started to softly hum a melody, her voice as gentle as her hands that stroked Cara's face.

"But who's going to protect us from him?" Cara asked drowsily as her eyes closed and she drifted off into a peaceful sleep.

Beckett watched as Feya cared for Cara like a guardian angel, the song she hummed filled him with calm, like a warm drink soothing all the way down.

"Does this happen to her often?' Beckett asked Feya.

"Not too often," Feya replied, "Sometimes it just gets to be too much, she's not as strong as she pretends to be."

"I know that." Beckett said, "She needs to stop trying to take care of everything herself."

"She tries to keep it together for Ferris and me, she's never had anyone to care for her, she's only ever had herself to rely on for so long that she doesn't know how to be any other way." Feya ran a finger over the bruised skin on Cara's temple, "the Supernaturals have always been hard on her."

"Why is that? I get the fact that everyone is drawn to her, but why do they want to hurt her when they get there?" Beckett asked as he took a seat in the desk chair.

Feya stood and clicked off the bedside lamp and then sat on the opposite side of the bed next to Cara. "Well unlike your group and Ferris and I who want to find her, the rest of the beings out there are being drawn to her against their will. I know you can't feel it for some reason, but it's like you don't even know it's happening, it's completely unconscious." Feya settled back against some pillows she'd propped up, "Like the guys out there in the woods tonight, they will still feel her pull but because they are aware of it, they will be able to hold it off for a while, but it does seem the longer you try to fight it, the stronger the lure will become."

"Then how does she ever get away from them?"

"It seems to be a distance thing. The only way Cara has found to be useful against being found, is to keep moving. She can sense supernatural's from two hundred miles away, we know because we've done experiments to find out what the boundaries were and the farther away they are, the less potent her pull seems to be, so we move to constantly keep the beings at bay."

"Why do you only stay in Ireland then? Wouldn't it be better to move from country to country?"

"After all these years Cara pretty much knows where all the super's tend to be, she's been to other countries but it's just too dangerous, bigger countries, a bigger congregation of beings. Here in our home country, we know the areas and landscapes and when we keep moving and can pretty successfully avoid detection."

Beckett thought about that for a moment, "where do you get your money from? It's obvious you can't work if you have to move every few days."

Feya smiled up at him from where she sat on the bed, "You forget one of our travelling companions is a leprechaun, money's never been a concern for us."

Beckett chuckled softly at that as he watched Cara sleep.

"You care for her don't you?' Feya asked him, he lifted his emerald eyes to her trusting brown ones, "I can tell by how you watch her." Beckett didn't respond and Feya knew her assumptions were right. "It's strange that you can't feel her lure. I wonder if you are the only person in the world who wouldn't have ever found Cara… if you hadn't been seeking her."

Beckett wasn't comfortable going down the path their conversation was headed, "How did you end up finding her?" he asked instead.

"I didn't find her…" Feya smiled softly down at Cara's restful face, "she found me."

This was it, Caleb had felt it all day, the moon was full and he was ready. The last dregs of amber from the sun sinking below the horizon faded, and the sky turned dark blue. He knew they wouldn't be able to fight it off much longer, and at this point he didn't want to anymore. The night was quiet, and clear, no stars speckled the indigo curtain overhead, just the bright giant orb of power shining down on him as he made his way into the cover of trees, Spike and Oliver not far behind him.

All of his senses were heightened. He could see through the darkness, his dilated pupils could see every blade of grass, their minute movement in the cool night breeze. He could faintly heard the conversation from in the hotel room, the light from their window dissolving as he disappeared under the trees. The earthy smell of the lush vegetation tingled his nostrils; he picked up the mingled scents of people from where they had traveled down the worn path to the lake. He paused where the path veered off to the left, but turned right, ducking under the low, leafy braches and into the thick underbrush.

As he walked farther into the forest, he unbuttoned his shirt and left it where it fell on the ground behind him, the misty air felt cool on his bare chest. Off to his right he could hear the rapid heartbeat of some small critter, probably a squirrel scampering around in the trees; his muscles bunched and he quickened his pace. He could feel Spike and Oliver spreading out on either side of him. He unbuckled his belt and dropped his trousers, stepping out of them he began to run, his bones on fire, craving the freedom to release his beast. Faster and faster he pumped his long legs, his feet pounded the ground, breath panted, heart raced, he burst through the trees into a small clearing and felt the moons lucent beams touch his sweat glazed skin like a caress; he arched his back and lifted his fists to the sky as his body started to mold, his muscles morphed, bones reconstructed, Caleb let out a yell which ended in a howl as four paws hit the ground.

The sudden drop from seven feet to four feet was always a bit disconcerting, the perspective was so much different, but Caleb sometimes felt more comfortable at this height. He took a shallow breath then snuffed it out his nostrils, testing the air for scents. Spike and Oliver were close, he could hear them coming. Flexing his paws he felt the rich soil spread up around his claws, swishing his tail along the ground he was unconsciously leaving his scent here, marking his territory.

Peering down his long muzzle, out over his black nose he watched Spike trot out of the bushes to his left, Oliver came from his right, having done their change as well. Both their fur was sandy, blonde and much shorter than his own deep brown fur, but it was always easy to tell the brothers apart; Spike was slightly shorter than Oliver and much shorter than Caleb who, when on all fours, stood five inches above Oliver, but Spike's girth out did them both.

They made their way over to where Caleb stood in the middle of the moonlit glen, yipping with excitement Spike bounced around Oliver, trying to provoke him into a tussle. Indifferent Oliver sidestepped his brother's antics but a little nip on his tail from Spike's sharp front teeth started the chase.

With what equals a chuckle in wolf language, Caleb sat on his haunches and watched in amusement as Oliver chased Spike around the clearing, finally overtaking him, Oliver pounced and tackled Spike to the ground. In a cloud of dust they wrestled, teeth snapping, trying to pin each other to the grass, one would gain the upper hand just to be bucked off or out maneuvered, Oliver had just got Spike by the throat and had him pinned when they smelled it, a deer. Standing up, Caleb gazed off through the dark trees in front of him, he couldn't see it, but he could smell it on the air that drifted under his nose, ears twitching trying to pick up any sound. Sensing Caleb's alertness the brothers stopped playing and came to stand beside him. They couldn't talk when in wolf form but they could read each other's body language and Caleb as their Alpha always took the lead. Without a look, Caleb darted off and plunged into the woods, with a wild howl Spike took off after him, Oliver taking up the rear.

Caleb ran, his strong legs carrying him over bushes and his keen senses dodging trees and carrying him in pursuit of his prey, he was all instincts now, no thought of his human self entered his mind, he was all wolf tonight. Skidding to a halt just before a barrier of briars, he knew the deer was on the other side of them. With a look he sent Oliver and Spike around to flank and come up behind the deer, they've hunted together so many times they knew the routine, and reveled in it every time.

Feeling they were each in place, Caleb stepped over the brambles and came face to face with the giant red stag. He was big, his age showing on his huge antlers, the fear showing in his eyes, being face to face with a predator. Caleb lowered his body as he crouched down in the tall grass his prey had been munching on moments ago, his eyes on the deer's, the smell of fear was intoxicating.

They stood staring at one another, the deer surprised and unsure until he heard Spike tramping through the brush from behind, then he took off at a gallop. Baring his teeth in a grin, Caleb started after his prey, this was what he'd wanted, the pursuit, the hunt. Keeping the deer in his sight, he followed him closely as he bounded through the dark forest, sprinting around trees as if they weren't even there; the deer beat a path back towards the lake. Knowing that they had to stop the deer before he reached the lake Spike lunged for his hindquarters but missed and stumbled, fell back, Caleb increased his pace. If the deer reached the lake before they stopped him he could be home free, they didn't want a kill so close to where people would be fishing and boating tomorrow. He heard Spike catching up to his rear, when off from the right Oliver darted out of the bushes and caught the deer in its side, sending them tumbling to the ground.

Spike leapt on top of the flailing deer and sunk his claws into his rear flank, the deer crying out, his eyes rolling back in panic, still fighting to gain his feet again, but Caleb came around front of him while Spike and Oliver held him down, and ripped out his throat. The kill was clean and quick and after a few last struggles the deer was dead. The wolves sat back from their kill as he bled out on the dark green forest floor, Caleb always insisted they give a moment of silence in appreciation of the life that was given for them before they started to feed.

Chapter 18

CARA COULDN'T REMEMBER FALLING ASLEEP. She'd just closed her eyes for a second but when she opened them again she was no longer in the little hotel room. She was in a great golden chariot, pulled by two large, white cats. They led her along the base of the clouds as they drifted through the sky. Cara felt the silken reigns in her hands and the armor that sheathed her body. Long golden locks of hair under a winged helmet wavered in the wind behind her as she rode through the sky and the weight of a ruby pendant hung heavy around her neck. Her shoulders were bare except for the two thin straps that held the breastplates around her chest. Rows of leather lames ringed her narrow waist then tapered off at her hips where a coarse woolen skirt fluttered above her knees; an iron shield was strapped to her left forearm and a leather scabbard held an ivory sword at her side.

The magnificent white cats drew her chariot through the last barrier of clouds, the moisture dappling her cheeks as they dove down. Cara watched as they broke through from the heavens then stopped, hovering high above the ground below. She was without fear for she knew where she was; this was her place, her duty she thought as she looked down at the battle waging on the field below.

The sky was gloomy on this side of the clouds, almost as if the sun couldn't bear to watch the cruelty of war. But war was part of every life force, whether they were god or human, they always found a reason to fight, destiny would have it no other way.

Cara watched and listened as the men fought beneath her floating chariot, the sounds of turmoil was like music to her ears. She didn't have to wonder who would come out the victor, because she'd already decided.

The mortals would march to fight for their freedoms, their lands, their loved ones who waited at home with bated breath, but their fates had already been determined, the warp and weft of life had already been wove.

With a satisfied smile, the end of the battle was nigh; Cara turned and watched her flock of valkyries descend from the sky, swooping down astride their black, winged wolves to collect the souls of the bravest of warriors.

With a start Cara blinked and came suddenly awake; sitting up in bed she gazed around the bright room. The bed was huge, with high brass posts at its four corners, holding up the purple satin canopy overhead.

Something had startled her awake, she could tell something was wrong, swinging her feet off the side of the bed, the gauzy, white fabric of her gown swished around her ankles, her blonde hair hung in a braid down her back.

Cara scanned the room but no one was there. The sun shone brightly in through the windows but a darkness still lurked behind the light. Slowly she padded, barefoot around the room, nothing seemed out of place. She stopped in front of a mirror, it stretched twenty feet up the stone wall but wide enough for only her to stand before it. She delighted in her own beauty, hair like liquid gold, eyes as blue as the southern sea and skin softer than a harp song.

Sighing contentedly she turned in front of the mirror, examining every angle, her hands gliding down her body and feeling her sensuous curves when she realized the weight around her neck was missing. With a gasp she reached up to her chest where the necklace always hung but it was gone. "He's stolen it!" she cried out. Furious she clenched her fists at her side and screamed until her lungs hurt.

A man burst through the door, his sword drawn, "What is it my lady?" he asked, his eyes searching for the danger.

Cara stamped her foot against the cold marble floor and whirled on him, her eyes seething and her cheeks flushed. "He's stolen the Brisling! My necklace is gone!"

The guard looked at her unadorned neck then quickly shouted, "Who has done this my lady?"

"That fiend Loke!" she cried, "He has stolen it. Go and find him and bring my necklace back!"

The bright bedroom faded before her eyes and materialized in a meadow, Cara was running, her sandaled feet slapping the ground, her necklace thumping against her clavicle. She'd seen him fall just ahead, her beloved was dying, murdered by her master and she had to get to him.

Seeing his crumpled body lying in the tall grass she hurried over to him and knelt down beside him.

"Oh, my love, don't leave me." Cara turned his face toward her and rested his head on her lap.

He opened his eyes to see her beautiful face one more time, "I knew I wouldn't be able to keep you forever." he whispered gently.

Shaking her head Cara tried to deny that this was happening, she cried tears of red gold that dripped off her cheeks and fell onto his, he smiled then took his last breath. Seeing that he was gone, Cara wailed and clutched his body to her breast, her hair a blanket over his pierced chest and the sorrow ripping a matching wound in her heart.

She felt cold and dead inside, when she finally stopped crying and stood up, vengeance an icy dagger in her side. Reaching up to her neck, she stroked the amber encased ruby pendant, her hands covered in her husband's blood.

Cara watched as her wolves came to her from across the meadow, they would exact her revenge and Odin would pay for what he'd done.

The largest wolf leading the pack stopped in front of her, his massive head as high as her chest, jade coloured eyes inquiring softly of his mistress what she would have him do.

Reaching out to the giant beast Cara twined her fingers through the soft mane of fur around his face, stroked down his neck and over his withers to where his black feathered wings lay flat against his back. She rested her forehead against his and brought her hands up under his ears, one last tear slipped between her closed eyelids and dripped down the wolf's muzzle.

He whimpered softly at sensing his mistress' sorrow and nuzzled her face.

"My loyal servant," she whispered against his black fur, "my ever faithful child. Ood my beloved is dead, killed at the hand of my lord and master Odin, whom we've all served for an eternity, ferrying souls to his hall to create his precious einherjar warriors. But this act of evil can not go without penalty." Standing back from the wolf she stroked the necklace around her throat and proclaimed in a loud voice, "I grant you the ability to change into human form. Go to Valhalla in disguise, but once you are inside revert back to your true form and avenge my husband's death."

Her voice still echoed across the field when the head wolf transformed into a man, he stood towering over her, bronzed skin and long black hair framing his face, only by his eyes could Cara recognize him as her wolf.

In a ripple of reformation, one by one the multitude before her changed from beast to man and she was pleased. Dropping her hand away from her necklace, Cara lifted her arms to the sky and called for the clouds to blot out the light, the sun would not shine in Asgard this day. Charging her army, they marched from the meadow, leaving her husband dead in the grass.

The sky boiled angrily overhead as they advanced on Odin's court in Valhalla. The enormous crystal tower speared through the clouds, the wind grew cold and thunder rumbled the heavens. Her wolves as men strode through the guarded gates unimpeded and entered Odin's sacred hall. Once across the threshold the wolves changed back into their bestial forms, spreading their wings they plunged down off the balconies over the sleeping einherjar in the courtyard below.

Cara entered the tower last; chaos reigned as her wolves brutally destroyed Odin's warriors. Leaning over the railing, Cara watched as the einherjar, having been taken by surprise and completely unprepared for the attack, most succumbed to her wolves, a few managing to grab their weapons and fight back.

With sadistic joy she reveled in the screams of the warriors, the sounds of tearing flesh, blood splattering and marring Odin's perfect palace walls, she felt no remorse when one of her wolves were wounded or killed, their cries couldn't penetrate her hate filled heart. Lifting her eyes, she gazed across the hall to where Odin stood on an opposite balcony. Horror and anguish contorted his face as he watched his warriors die.

"Freyja, forgive me!" he wailed, "He tricked me." Odin cried wretchedly then flung himself off the balcony into the turmoil below.

Lightning struck outside the tower; the earth began to quake as Cara looked at Odin's mangled body where it had landed on the crystal floor, a pool of scarlet spreading out around him. She saw her wolf with the jade green eyes stare up at her from next to his dying corpse, blood sputtered out of his lips.

"Finish it." she whispered. The wolf lowered his head to Odin's and clamped his jaws around his neck, growling he snapped it clean off and with the great gods head dangling bloody from his powerful mouth, he tossed it into a heap on his dead warriors bodies.

It was done; Cara thought and turned her eyes from the carnage. She could hear screams, but they were coming from outside the hall since the fighting inside had stopped. The walls shook and began to break apart as giant masses of fire and ice rained over the kingdom, the surviving einherjar and wolves fled from the crumbling courtyard. Cara peered out the window, Asgard was falling, clutching her necklace she ripped it from her neck; she knew this was the end of the kingdom of the gods. Holding the necklace outside the window she dropped it just as the final footholds of Valhalla broke and the crystal palace tumbled down around her.

Cara could feel nothing anymore, but she watched the necklace, its amber chains dangling as it plummeted through the sky, the ruby stone flashing red then green, then black, then gold, then blue, as it fell, the earth rushing up to meet it.

JUST BEFORE THE NECKLACE smashed into the earth Cara gasped awake and jolted upright in bed, her eyes meeting Beckett's where he sat in the desk chair across the room.

"What is it?" he demanded anxiously and rushed to her side. Cara's breath heaved heavily out of her lungs, cold sweat dripped from her forehead and down her back; Beckett gripped her face in his hands and turned her wild eyes to face him.

She focused on his emerald eyes to calm herself, "They're here." she announced in a hoarse whisper.

Chapter 19

"WHO'S HERE?" BECKETT ASKED. TRYING to get Cara to calm down so he could figure out what the problem was? She pushed his hands away and leapt off the bed.

"They've all finally found me." Cara said, her voice quivering as she tried to get control of the fear.

"What's going on?" Feya asked as she woke from her spot on the bed next to where Cara had been lying.

"There's hundreds of them!" Cara exclaimed in disbelief, "they're all around us, completely surrounding the hotel."

"You mean supernatural's?" Beckett asked, Cara turned to him and nodded. He moved to the window and peered around the drawn curtain, Cara crowded next to him to see for herself.

"Just look at them all, how did they all manage to get here at once? They must have come from miles." Cara observed the eerie scene just outside the hotel room. The moon still shone in its fullness overhead, in its beams she could see the figures of dozens of beings, male, female, every mixture of races, all standing deadly still, like zombies. Cara shivered at the comparison, "What do you think they're doing?" she asked, gazing up at Beckett. She could see his jaw muscles were clenched in concentration.

"Look at their eyes." he instructed, and Cara looked back out the window.

She gasped, her hand going to her mouth, "Oh sweet Mother, they're all possessed." She closed her eyes. "Yes, I can sense it now, they all have that same black haze around them that Maureen had back at the bar. What are they waiting for?" she wondered.

Beckett turned quickly from the window, pulling Cara with him. He spun her around and sat her in the desk chair, his face close to hers, "I need to know how many there are and what kind of beings they are. What exactly are we up against?"

"There's a hundred, at least." she said, "and every kind of being, faeries, trolls, gnomes, even a werewolf or two, you name it, we've got it!"

"Cara, can you still see the boys out in the woods?' Feya asked concerned.

Cara closed her eyes, "Yes, they're still there, Gannon is moving closer to the hotel, maybe he saw them come."

"First thing we need to do is get out of this room, we can't fight them being surrounded like we are." Beckett moved to look back out the window when a fist broke through the pane, sending shattered glass everywhere.

Feya shrieked and disappeared, Cara grabbed her gun off the bedside table and shoved it down her waistband, holding her iron stake in her left hand she was ready to fight.

"How many are around the door?" Beckett asked.

"About fifteen and more closing in." Cara replied, she reached out into the air and grabbed Feya's hand that only she could see and tugged her up behind Beckett at the door.

"When I open this, you run and don't stop." Beckett counted to three then flung the door wide open, the force sent the clamoring bodies outside of it flying backwards. "Go!" Beckett yelled as he was swarmed.

Cara dashed out the door, taking advantage of the break in the mass of possessed supernaturals and pushed Feya ahead of her. Sensing Ferris running behind her, she stopped and grabbed him by the shirttails and tucked him under her arm and dashed for the cover of trees.

"What are they all doing here? They've all gone wacky." Ferris rambled as Cara tossed him unceremoniously to the ground next to Feya at the edge of the woods.

"Stay here!" she ordered the two of them and ran back into the melee. She couldn't see Beckett in the midst of the mob but she could sense him. Every being had converged on their location in a frenzy, like someone flicked a riot switch. Bodies clashed, and clawed, climbing over top each other trying to reach Beckett who was trying to fight his way out, but for everyone he threw off, two more descended.

Throwing herself at the crowd she brandished her iron blade and slashed and stabbed any part of any creature she could reach. Battling them back she slowly picked her way to where Beckett was fighting a grogoch, normally these faeries were very sociable and always trying to be helpful but the little creature had his feet braced on Beckett's stomach and his claws wrapped around his throat, his eyes blazing red.

Cara stabbed the hairy creature in his leg, he screamed in pain at the iron cutting his flesh and let go of Beckett.

"Come on." she called and started to run back towards the trees but it was no use. They were forced to stop when they saw the supernatural army regrouping. Cara and Beckett stood back-to-back, circling; they were almost completely surrounded again.

"Well now what?" she asked.

Before Beckett could answer, Caleb burst into the yard, followed by Spike, Oliver and Gannon.

"Gannon saw them circling the building so he came and got us." Caleb explained out of breath as they jogged over to Beckett and Cara; he'd only had time to pull on his trousers, his chest was still bare. "Is Feya safe?" he asked, not taking his eyes off the gathering demons.

"She and Ferris are hiding in the woods." Cara told him.

"Holy crap, there's so many of them!" Spike exclaimed, his muscles tensed as he crouched in a fighter's stance.

"What are we going to do?" Oliver asked as he flanked Caleb's left side.

"No time to find out." Gannon said as the demon closest to him lunged.

They charged as a group against the oncoming throng, but they were outnumbered and outgunned against the vast variety of supernatural powers the adversaries had at their disposal. No matter how many times they fought them down, they'd get right back up, advancing again.

"This is ridiculous!" Gannon shouted as he slammed a ham fisted troll into the ground, clumps of dirt flew up from the impact.

"They won't stop coming as long as they are possessed." Caleb said, wiping blood from the corner of his mouth.

"Can you exorcise them?" Cara asked.

"I can try, but they need to be pinned down." Caleb drew the medallion from his pants pocket. Oliver tackled the faerie he'd been fighting to the ground and held him there as best he could, the rest of them trying to hold back the rest of them.

As Caleb started reading the incantation, the demons lost it, turned savage, psychotically tearing and attacking. Beckett fell to the ground as one slashed open his chest, his shirt blossomed red and Cara ran to help him but before she could get to him he'd kicked the demon off and jumped up.

"Are you okay?" Frantically Cara spread his torn shirt and felt through the blood to see how bad the cut was, but under her fingers she only felt smooth skin.

"We heal fast remember?"

Cara looked up at his blood-smeared face without a scratch on it. "Lucky for you then." Cara shoved him away slightly and turned back to where Caleb was knelt on the ground next to the flailing demon, when another werewolf who'd been possessed, leapt through the air and landed on Caleb's back. Cara wasn't sure at first what he was; he'd changed only the top half of his body to that of a wolf but still retained the legs of a man. Cara started running but it was too late. Just as Caleb spoke the last words of the exorcism the wolf-man reared back his head and sunk his sharp fangs into Caleb's shoulder.

Caleb roared in pain and bucked the werewolf off his back, while Oliver tossed aside the disoriented faerie he'd been holding down and ran to Caleb, his own face battered and bloody, nose broken, he helped him stand and supporting his weight he lead Caleb to the trees.

"That's enough of this!" Spike hollered furiously, his chest was riddled with nasty gashes that wouldn't heal as fast as Beckett's had, his right arm hung oddly at his side. With his left hand he picked up the limp right one and tucked it tight against his stomach, then with a twist and a loud pop he snapped the dislocated shoulder back into its socket. With a menacing growl Spike pounced on the wolf-man that had attacked Caleb, transforming his hands into paws as he charged and raked his claws across the wolf's throat as he came down on him. Blood sprayed Spike's face as his head fell back, only holding on by a thin flap of skin and a big cloud of black smoke exited out of the wound.

Stunned Cara stood looking at the dead werewolf, another possessed faerie came from behind and knocked Spike to the ground. Oliver ran out from where'd he'd left Caleb under the trees and snapped its neck, the demon smoking from its lifeless body.

"No!" Cara screamed. She watched in horror as puffs of demons smoke expelled out of the fallen beings. She saw a faerie about to attack Beckett and the dead bodies lying at his feet. Cara stepped in front of Beckett and shoved him back, "You can't kill them!" she yelled at him. The faerie who was aiming at Beckett stuck Cara instead, the force sending her twisting through the air and thudding hard against the base of a tree ten feet away.

Enraged, Beckett grabbed the faerie that was flying at him again and yanked his arm until he heard it snap. He turned to where Cara was coughing on her hands and knees; blood drenched her hair from a large gash on the back of her head. Caleb and Feya rushed over to her, "Make sure she stays out of this." Beckett commanded Caleb who was gripping a piece of cloth to his torn shoulder, he nodded and knelt down next to Cara to examine her head wound and Beckett turned back to the fight.

Cara couldn't focus, every muscle in her body ached, she felt a warm dampness running down her back.

"Cara, look at me." She tried to zero in on Feya's voice, but she sounded so far away.

"Is she okay?" Feya asked Caleb.

"It isn't as bad as it looks, head wounds bleed a lot more." Caleb said. He removed the blood soaked cloth from his shoulder; the jagged edges of skin around the bite marks were already starting to knit themselves back together. As he stood up to rejoin the fight, Cara reached out and grabbed the hem of his trousers.

"You can't kill them. Please." she begged him, but he shook his head sadly and walked away, leaving Feya to comfort her.

Cara cried out in anguish, the tears streaming down her face as she closed her eyes and watched each individual light of colour fade away.

Chapter 20

THE BATTLE ENDED QUICKLY WHEN the demons realized they were no longer playing nicely, many retreated, but too many had needed to die.

Caleb stood next to Beckett, their faces solemn and both covered in blood, as they surveyed the decimation. Twenty-five dead supernaturals lay strewn around the back of the old, yellow hotel building. He hadn't been ready for this, for the loss of life the pure carnage that war creates. And this was war, he finally realized, Loke was playing for keeps and obviously they were in his way.

Oliver returned from walking the perimeter of the property, checking to make sure all the ones who had fled were really gone, he brought back with him the faerie that had struck Cara; his arm was badly broken but he was still alive.

I caught this one crawling off into the woods." Oliver said as he marched his prisoner up to Caleb and Beckett. "Figured you might want to talk to him."

Caleb observed the faerie being made to stand before him, it was hard to see past the angelic face and into the demon inside, but his eyes flashed an angry red as he snarled up at him.

"Why were you sent to find us?" Caleb inquired of him.

The faerie spat at Caleb's face but being so much shorter than him, it only reached his collarbone.

Still holding his hands behind his back, Oliver forced the faerie to his knees in the grass, "Watch yourself." he warned. "Now answer the question."

"My master sent us; his will be done." the demon proclaimed proudly.

"Where is he?" Caleb asked.

The demon laughed fiendishly, "You will never know that, you and your menagerie of misfits are of little significance to him, nothing but a meager aberration on our road to the final reckoning."

"If we're of such little importance to Loke, then why has he gone through so much trouble to get rid of us?" Beckett shot back.

"You are not fit to speak his name." the demon snarled at Beckett, "You won't be a problem much longer, your time is running out, the end is near, and when my master finds her and has the brisling in his hands, victory will…" Gannon came up behind him and with one quick jerk snapped his neck, releasing the demon in a billow of smoke; the faerie slumped forward, dead.

Cara saw him die from where she knelt at the edge of the forest; agony ripped a fresh wound in her heart. Pulling herself up to her feet she ran the few meters across the blood stained grass and launched herself at Gannon, "How could you!" she screamed as her fists pounded on his chest.

Gannon caught her wrists in his hands but she jerked them out of his grasp, Beckett steadied her as she stumbled back. "Get away from me!" she yelled and whirled to face them all, "How could you?!" she accused, angry tears burning her cheeks. "How could you just murder them all?"

"They were possessed Cara." Caleb spoke softly, his voice sorrowful.

"Exactly!" she shot back at him, "They were possessed, these beings had no control over what the demon inside them was making them do."

"What would you rather have had us do?" Spike asked belligerently. "Invite them in for tea and just politely ask them to please stop trying to kill *us*?!"

"When you kill the being that is being possessed, you're not killing the demon or even sending him back to the underworld, right?" Cara spun on Caleb.

"That's right." he agreed, "when you kill its host, the demon just gets released back into the air until it can find a replacement one." Caleb ran his hands through his hair and sighed.

"We were taken by surprise tonight, we can't let that happen again." Beckett stated.

"I didn't even know that Supernaturals could be possessed by demons, but now we do and that means that none of us are safe from that possibility either." Caleb thought aloud.

"This isn't going to be the last time something like this happens." Beckett said, "And we got lucky this time around even though we were greatly out numbered. But Loke knows this now and next time there will be more."

"Lucky?" Cara asked scornfully. "How can you call this lucky?" she spread her arms wide, taking in the span of dead bodies around them. "We need to find another way to fight this."

There is no other way." Gannon commented testily.

"I hate to agree with the bloodsucker but he's right." Spike piped up, "It's not like we can ask the rampaging demons to stand still for few minutes so Caleb can perform an exorcism on each of their asses." He rolled his right shoulder joint, and was annoyed at the clicking he heard on every downward rotation. "In case you haven't noticed, this is a war we're fighting here."

"So what? Neither of you care how many innocents get killed along the way?" Cara demanded, her golden eyes flashed violently.

"Unfortunately in a war, collateral damage is necessary." Caleb said, more to himself than anyone else, Cara rounded on him, but his haunted eyes were staring off into the distance.

I thought you hated them all anyway." Gannon said, crossing his arms, "You've spent your whole life running from them, I would have assumed a few less beings in the world would be a plus."

"They have no choice!" she exclaimed. "It isn't their choice to be drawn to me, just as they have no choice in being possessed and that shouldn't equal a death sentence." She turned to look at Feya who was hovering just outside the circle, "If we're not fighting for the innocent, then just what the hell *are* we fighting for?" Cara stood in front of the group, breathing hard from agitation, "Something has to matter. They have to matter." she pointed to the dead at their feet, "If not, then I say let Loke come."

Feya walked around to stand beside Cara. Ferris trundled out of the shadows where he'd been hiding and stood behind them, Cara was glad for their support.

Caleb looked over at the three huddled together and realized that their group could be seconds away from disbanding and then where would they all be?

"I think we can all agree that we have too many enemies to waste energy fighting each other." Caleb said, trying to speak reason. "The attacks are growing exponentially and we are not prepared. We all want to avoid hurting the innocent as best we can, but as Spike said, we are at war. It is unfortunate that our enemy is using the innocent to get to us, it shows he's a coward."

Beckett nodded his agreement. "But we need to protect ourselves for the greater good and we all need to be prepared to deal with the fact that people are going to get hurt and even killed."

Caleb saw Cara about to object but interrupted, "It's obvious that individual exorcisms will not work in a situation like we've faced here tonight, but I do recall hearing about a mass exorcism, one that when preformed will send all the demons within speaking range back to hell."

"Really?" Cara asked him, looking hopeful.

"I've never done it and don't know the specifics of it; I'll have to see if I can research it and I'll give a call to Lucille back in New York, if anyone will know about it, she will." Caleb replied. Turning to face the entire group as one, his back to the moon he said, "But none of this will be for anything as long as we are divided amongst ourselves, we all need to get on the same page and start working together toward the same end, we've got a lot worse things ahead of us." Caleb looked at his shoulder that had almost completely healed, "I think it's obvious that we can't stay in one place for too long."

"I'll leave." Cara said, "As long as I am with you, they will always be able to find us."

"No." Beckett said firmly. Cara glared at him but he spoke to Caleb, "She's not going anywhere alone."

"Beckett's right, Cara." Caleb acceded. "We're stronger when we're all together and I think we're on to something." He looked down at the dead faerie at his feet. "But for right now we need to clean up, then pack and get out of here."

"The sun will be up soon," Beckett observed the lightening sky, "Cara, if you and Feya would pack up all of our stuff and load the cars, the boys and I will take care of the bodies."

"What are you going to do with them?" she asked.

Beckett surveyed the dead bodies lying on the blood soaked ground. "We'll sink them in the lake. Unfortunately there is nothing we can do about the blood but we don't want the hotel owners to wake up to a field of dead supernaturals."

Cara looked back at the darkened hotel. "Do you really think they slept through all that?" she asked skeptically as she thought about the elderly couple that ran the hotel.

"It is doubtful, even more reason for us to get out of here quickly."

Cara took Feya and Ferris back to the hotel and began gathering up their things and shoving them in suitcases. After doing a onceover of their room to make sure they hadn't forgotten anything, they moved on to Caleb, Spike and Oliver's room.

Once they'd loaded all the bags into the two cars, Cara grabbed one of Caleb's shirts from his suitcase then went to find the others. All the bodies were now gone from the field; she walked across the yard and under the canopy of trees, down the path that lead to the lake. Reaching the end of the trail she saw Gannon, Oliver and Caleb standing around the edge of the lake. She moved up next to Caleb and handed him his shirt. He thanked her and slipped it on. Beckett and Spike were in the water, hauling the last two bodies out to the middle of the lake.

Cara looked at the bodies floating like macabre buoys on top of the black water and shivered. "How are you going to make them sink?" she asked.

Caleb winced slightly at the question, but never took his eyes off the lake. "We had to puncture the bodies."

"You stabbed them!" Cara asked incensed.

Caleb looked at her horror filled eyes. "We had to."

"Couldn't you have just weighed them down with something?"

"A dead body will naturally sink on it's own," Caleb explained, turning his gaze back out to Beckett and Spike working in the water. "But once they start to decompose the body will fill with gases making it rise to the surface again, dragging whatever weight we use with it. Puncturing holes in the corpses will prevent the gases from building up, it was the safest choice."

Spike and Beckett swam back to the shore and dripping came to stand next to the group. As one, they all watched in silence as one by one, the bodies began to sink below the surface. When the last one disappeared out of sight, they all turned and headed back down the path as the morning sun blinked over the treetops.

Chapter 21

BECKETT DROVE CARA'S OLD JETTA while she sat in the passenger's seat, Ferris was in his usual spot in the trunk, while Feya slept curled up in the back seat; Caleb and the others followed behind them in the SUV.

They'd been traveling for four hours in silence. Cara felt completely drained, like a stopper had been pulled and all the life had leaked out of her, there was nothing left inside anymore. She watched the beautiful green scenery flash by outside the window, they'd just entered Connemara and were passing through the old Quaker town of Letterfrack. They'd decided they should avoid staying in public places if they could and Cara knew of an old uninhabited farmhouse way out in the bog lands that would serve their purpose well.

"Turn left here." Cara directed Beckett as they came to the edge of town. Steering the car off the main road and onto a dirt one that seemed more appropriate for walking than driving, he held the car steady as they bumped along, the SUV following. As they drove along the road got worse and the trees thinned out. On either side of the road stretched plains of bogs hugging the rippling ground like a blanket, chunks of turf stood propped up against one another like tiny teepee's drying in the sun.

"It's not much farther." Cara said. She could see in the distance the Twelve Bens Mountains rising up around the town of Clifden like a bowl. As they rounded the last bend in the road, which had become just muddy wheel ruts in the peat, the tiny cabin came into view. Beckett pulled the car up beside it and turned off the engine. Feya stretched languorously awake in the back seat then joined the rest of them outside the car.

"You call that a road?" Spike grumbled as he slammed out of the SUV.

"What! Your big SUV couldn't handle it?" Beckett taunted.

"Please!" Spike retorted, "Another few minutes of that and we were sure that little bucket of bolts you were driving would shake apart right in front of our eyes."

"This is it." Cara pointed to the old stone building, the white paint was peeling off the outside walls and the thatched roof needed repair. "It's not much to look at but it'll suffice." She led the way to the front door, pulling her keys from her pocket she flipped through them until she found the right one and unlocked the heavy wooden door.

They stepped inside. It was dim and smelled stale. Cara walked to the two small windows and threw open the canvas curtains that hung over the dirty panes. Dust danced about in the beams of light that managed to shine through the grime on the windows.

The entire house was one level, the ceilings so low that Caleb had to tilt his head sideways to stand up. The main room they were standing in was the kitchen, dining room, and sitting room all in one. An ancient wood stove stood over to the right side of the room next to a sink with a pump handle and a metal icebox next to that. A stone fireplace took up most of the wall in front of the door, an antique rose-coloured couch sat in front of it, and a scarred wooden table was placed off to the left, with four mismatched chairs around it.

"There's no electricity or telephone of course, the roof leaks when it rains and a mighty draft seeps through the stone walls, but the pump in the sink does still work. There are two bedrooms through that door there by the fireplace." Cara explained as she moved around the room. "We do get cell phone service here so Caleb, if you have one you can make your calls back to the States from here, if not you'll have to go into town."

"Yes, we do have one." Caleb replied, "We keep it turned off for the most part because of the GPS tracking device in it, we never want to make it easy for people to follow us, but I guess that point is pretty much moot now."

"Yah, it pretty much is, when you've got a big old tracking device right here that can't be turned off."

Beckett watched as Cara slumped down on the couch and closed her eyes, he could see the exhaustion and defeat in her face and decided it was time to take control.

"Spike, go get the bags from the cars and bring them in, see what we have for bedrooms and assign people their sleeping arrangements." Spike nodded then headed back out to the cars. "We'll need some provisions; Oliver, make a list of supplies you think we'll need, then you and Feya go back into town, don't forget some ice for the icebox so we can keep some things cold. Gannon," Beckett turned to him, "I want you to scout out the area around the house and see what the hunting potential is, now that our blood supply is gone, we'll need to hunt tonight." Beckett turned back to Feya and Oliver, "Would you be able to pick up some small containers for us, something air tight and that we can fit in the ice box." Feya gulped audibly but nodded yes. "If you can't find anything suitable then Ziploc bags will have to do. Caleb, you've got phone calls to make? Good." When every one had their marching orders and set about their tasks, Beckett yanked Cara off the couch and pushed her out the door, "We're going for a walk." He announced to the house then shut the door behind them.

"WHAT IS THE MATTER with you?" Cara protested as he tucked her arm through his and started to walk.

Ignoring her protests Beckett held firm onto her hand and when she tried to tug it free, asked, "Is the house yours?"

"No." Cara shot back at him.

"But you have a key?" he pressed further.

"No one has lived here for as long as I can remember." she sighed, and gave up the futile attempts to get her hand free. "I discovered it years ago and we come by every few months. A few years back we found this old furniture on the side of the road in Letterfrack and brought it here." Cara said, "I have a key, because even though I know a locked door is really no security, even a false sense is better than none at all."

Her steps synced up with his as she started to relax and take in the scenery.

"Are there many super's around here?" he asked, letting go of her hand and was pleased when she didn't pull it away.

"Not too many actually." she told him, "Because this area is so barren with no trees and the peat bogs being constantly dug up for turf fuel, the beings tend to stay away." She closed her eyes for a second then looked up at him, "But I'm here now and they will come, but we should be okay for a few days."

They walked across the spongy ground, over the hills and past the rows of cut peat until they reached Sky Road, on one side was the town of Clifden, its cozy buildings nestled down amongst the shallow mountain peaks, the two stone church steeples peaking up into the sky. On the other side was the ocean; they jogged across the road and down the grassy knoll overlooking the rocky shore below.

"Do you want to go down to the beach?" Beckett asked her. But she shook her head, her chestnut hair bouncing in the breeze around her face.

"This is close enough." she smiled up at him, her golden eyes happy. "There are beings in the water too."

He was glad to see her finally at ease, the worry lines had smoothed out of her forehead and the fresh air had brought some colour back to her cheeks. "When did you first know there was something different about you?" he asked.

Surprised, she turned her gaze from the ocean up to him. "When I was three years old, I asked my Mother if she could see the pretty lights too. It was then I realized that not everyone could see the things I could." Cara lowered herself to the ground and crossed her legs Indian style. Grabbing Beckett's hand she tugged his down next to hers. "We moved around a lot, and it wasn't until Ma bought the house in Castleblayney that they started to find me."

"Were they always cruel to you?" Beckett asked softly.

"Not at first." she said, her eyes looking off into the distance as she thought back, "I'd see them when they'd actually physically show up, I could tell what they were, but they'd just stare at me, sort of confused, not really sure what to do and they'd leave." Cara gathered her hair back from her face and twisted it around her shoulder to hold it in place. "Until the day they came and took Alexia, I hadn't had too much trouble with the fair folk."

"Alexia? That was your sister? The one who was kidnapped?"

Cara nodded, "But it wasn't the way you're thinking. She was taken by a faerie and a changeling was left in her place." Cara told him how she'd taken the changeling and went in search of her baby sister but it had been too late. "That was the first time I'd met Feya, she saved my life that day." Cara smiled fondly back to that moment in time, Beckett thought it admirable that she could find some sweetness is such a devastating memory.

Sighing out of her thoughts Cara nudged him with her shoulder, "Now that you've asked your questions, I've some of my own."

He smiled over at her, his green eyes a bright spot against the grey sky, "Ask away." He invited and lay back in the grass, his hands under his head.

"Okay – why don't you drink human blood?" Cara flipped over to her stomach and lay down next to him, resting her cheek on her crossed arms so she could see his profile.

"I used to." he said after a moment.

"But what made you stop?"

"It was at the end of the first World War."

She propped herself up on her elbows, "You were in World War I?"

"I've been in many wars." he replied, tilting his head to look at her. "I fought with the French in the Battle of Agincourt, I watched Joan of arc burn at the stake. I won with Yorkshire in the War of the Roses and marched with the British Cavalry at Waterloo. I invaded under General Lee's command at Gettysburg and lost, but defeated Custer at Little Big Horn. And I fed on all my fallen enemies, until my last battle in WWI when the stench of human casualties finally left a bad taste in my mouth."

Cara's mouth gaped open, "You were in all those wars?"

Beckett nodded and turned his eyes back to the sky.

"You were a regular little mercenary weren't you?"

Beckett laughed bitterly, "I suppose I was. I always justified it by thinking that I was fighting evil and satisfying my needs for survival, but I realized that the humans and their petty wars don't fight evil, they create it and I was just fueling my own evil inside of me. So I ran away."

"And now you're back." Cara pointed out, "Ready to fight another war for the humans."

"Not just the humans." Beckett corrected her, "Every living thing on the earth will be affected by this."

Cara rolled over onto her back and stared silently up at the clouds, the gun she'd kept tucked in her waistband dug into the small of her back. Beckett turned his head to look at her; he was worried she would be afraid of him now, that she wouldn't be able to get over what he had been, what he had done. Sitting up, Beckett raked his hands through his hair then rested his arms on his knees while he looked at her over his shoulder, "What are you thinking?"

"Joan of Arc was executed in 1431 – "

Beckett nodded, a little confused, "Yes."

Cara's eyes met his, "How old *are* you?"

Beckett threw back his head and laughed with delight, the woman was a marvel, he thought, lowering himself over top of her and grinned mischievously, "How old do I look?"

Cara smiled and ran her hands up his strong arms that were braced on wither side of her body and grasped them behind his neck, "We all know looks can be deceiving."

Cara slowly closed her eyes as Beckett brought his face his down to hers, but stopped, his lips a hair's breadth from hers. "What's wrong?" she asked.

Beckett lowered his eyes to her neck, "You're wearing a cross." he said.

"Oh." Cara giggled softly and sat up a bit, "I forgot I'd put it on this morning." Grasping the chain she pulled it off over her head, her hair flipping up and again falling in place over her back, she looked down at the silver pendant in her hand. The cross has been shaped from metal strings woven together in intricate Celtic knots. "It used to be my Mother's. This necklace was all they'd been able to recover…" Cara trailed off.

"What is it?" Beckett asked, he saw her nose crinkle the way it did whenever she was trying to figure something out.

"A necklace." she said, "The Brisling is a necklace." Cara jumped to her feet.

"What are you talking about?" Beckett asked bewildered as he stood up.

"The Brisling, he mentioned it, the demon said that Loke was looking for it, for her." Cara started to pace excitedly, still looking at the necklace in her hand.

"For who? What demon?" Beckett grabbed Cara's hand and brought her to stand still in front of him.

Cara sighed impatiently, "The demon Oliver captured last night, the one Caleb questioned before Gannon killed him."

"What about him?"

"He said that his master was looking for someone, and when he found her, whoever she is, he would find the Brisling, remember?"

"Okay, yes, I remember, but how do we know that actually means anything? He's a demon, not exactly trustworthy."

"No, but it make perfect sense! I thought at first he meant me, when he said Loke was looking for someone, but that can't be right because he knows where to find me, I can't hide, so it has to be someone or something else that Loke wants." Cara exclaimed, "When I was sleeping, before I sensed all the possessed supernaturals surrounding the hotel, I had been having a dream; it was so real. I was aware of myself but looking through the eyes of another, and living her life."

"Who was it?" he asked.

"I don't know for sure, but I think I was seeing through the eyes of Freyja, that Valkyrie Caleb told us about." Cara bounced eagerly.

"What makes you say that?" Beckett asked, placing his hands on her shoulders trying to hold her still.

"Because I saw everything Caleb described, I saw my valkyries riding their winged wolves into battle to collect the fallen souls, the souls that became Odin's einherjar, your ancestors."

"Okay." Beckett nodded slowly, trying to make sense of her rambling.

"It was Freyja, I know it was her, and she had a necklace. Oh it was beautiful, columns of amber gold around the neck and a huge pendant of rubies." Cara gestured around her neck as she tried to describe how the necklace had hung there. "She called the necklace, the Brisling!" Cara shouted. Beckett let her go and watched her walk in circles around him, talking rapidly as she tried to remember the dream.

"And I dreamt that Loke had stolen it and I- well, she was furious, but she somehow got it back. Then I flashed to a scene in the dream when her husband Ood was killed by Odin, remember Loke tricked him into it?" Without waiting for him to respond Cara continued, "As her husband died in her arms I felt her heart break, she used her necklace to call all the wolves to her then she used it to give them the ability to change forms."

"Why would Loke be looking for the necklace though?" Beckett asked.

"Don't you see? The necklace has the ability to control all the wolves, all the werewolves." Cara stopped when the realization struck her; she turned wide-eyed to Beckett. "He wants to control the werewolves to have them fight for him."

Cara closed her eyes and clutched a hand to her mouth, "I think I'm going to be sick." Beckett grabbed her and turned her to face him.

"Look at me." He ordered and she opened her eyes, all the colour the fresh air had put in her cheeks was gone. "We don't know if any of this is true, but we do need to talk to the others about it."

"Oh Beckett we can't let it happen." Cara cried and hugged him tightly around his waist; tears burned the back of her eyes as she thought about Caleb, Spike and Oliver. She didn't even want to consider what would happen if Loke found someway to control them. Beckett wrapped protective arms around her and held her close.

"We won't, we'll figure it out." Beckett said soothingly, "In your dream, did you see what she did with the Brisling?"

"When Asgard began to crumble and everyone began to flee, Freyja dropped the necklace and I watched it fall to the earth, but I don't know where, that was when I woke up." Cara pulled away from him so she could look at his face, "Do you think it could be here… on Earth?"

"I don't know." Beckett replied, "But I think the more important question is, who is this person Loke is looking for that he believes can find it for him?"

Chapter 22

BECKETT AND CARA PRACTICALLY RAN all the way back to the farmhouse from the ocean, the SUV wasn't parked in the yard.

"Oliver and Feya must still be in town." Beckett commented.

Cara stopped in front of the house and closed her eyes for a moment, "They must have all gone, I can't sense anyone here." she said disappointed. Checking again she scanned the neighboring town, "yes, they're still in town."

"They'll be back soon." Beckett reassured her, "Why don't you go find out where Spike put your stuff and unpack, I'm just going to go grab some of that turf we saw cut on the way in so we'll have a fire for tonight."

Cara walked inside the little cabin and across the seating area, through the door beside the fireplace. On the other side of the door was a small hall with two more doors, each leading into a small bedroom. Cara was about to open one door when she heard a voice coming from behind the other one.

Cara closed her eyes again to see if she'd somehow missed sensing someone but she couldn't see anyone there. They must be human, she thought. With her hand poised on the doorknob she leaned closer to the door to try to hear who was talking.

"I've looked Master, I can't find anything." Cara heard a man's voice whisper from inside the room. "I don't think Cara knows where she is-" At the mention of her name Cara reached for the gun tucked in her waist band, whoever it was obviously knew her, maybe another demon.

"There has to be another way to find her and I don't think I can be useful here any longer, the demon attack the other night almost cost us, I had to help them fight, or else they would have found out –" The voice trailed off, they were obviously talking to someone that Cara couldn't hear, on the phone maybe. "Yes my Lord. Thy will be done." Cara heard the snap of a cell phone closing shut, the conversation was over. She heard the person inside shuffling through papers, opening and closing drawers, whoever it was, was searching for something. Cara closed her eyes and checked for Beckett, he was still down the road a ways and she didn't have time to wait for him. Grasping the doorknob to the bedroom, she mentally counted to three then flung the door wide open.

The door bounced back against the wall with a thud as she swung into the room, her gun trained on the man who was bent over her open suitcase on the bed, his back to her.

"Don't move. I've a gun aimed right at you." she told him, "Put your hands in the air and turn around slowly."

The man stood up straight, lifting his hands up on either side of his head, he laughed sarcastically as he slowly turned around. Cara gasped in shock when she saw his face, her gun waivered slightly but she steadied it and aimed it higher.

"Now Cara, you know that won't do any good against me." Gannon regarded the gun she had trained at his head and smirked.

"You?" she accused stunned.

"Yes, me." Gannon retorted snidely, smoothing his slick black hair over his head then dropping his hands to his side.

"Who were you talking to?" Cara demanded as she saw his closed cell phone lying on the bed.

"The big guy himself." Gannon declared with enthusiasm, he took a step towards her, Cara stepped back.

"Loke? You're working for him?"

"You guessed it sweet cheeks."

"I can't sense you. How is that possible?"

"Ah yes, my little advantage." Gannon removed a small metal flask from his pants pocket and shook it, Cara heard liquid swishing around inside. "It's a serum my master had developed, it makes it impossible for you to sense me." Gannon moved closer to Cara, until her gun pressed right against his chest. "Remember the night after the demon attack at the bar and your blood smelled- "Gannon closed his eyes and breathed in through his nose then out on a moan, "so delicious?"

Cara glared at him, she'd never felt pure hatred before until now.

Her heart like it would pound out of her chest, not from fear, but from anger.

Gannon laughed wickedly, "and I went to *cool off*?" he emphasized with air quotes. "That was the first time I used it, worked like a charm."

"But I saw you that night, I sensed you walking around the town, then I saw you when you were on your way to the hotel." Cara reminded him.

"Yes, I'd only taken a sip and it doesn't last long, but it was long enough for me to kill that lovely college girl and suck her dry." Gannon said then laughed when he saw her eyes flash.

Cara remembered the newspaper headline they'd read the following morning; they'd wondered why out of all the other crimes that girl had been the only one to die.

Cara was about to pull the trigger she had aimed at his heart, even though it wouldn't do any good she wanted to hurt him in anyway she could, Beckett walked into the bedroom, her attention shifted for one second but it was enough. Gannon knocked Cara's arm, the gun went off but the bullet shot through the roof, he pulled her in front of him, his hand gripping tightly around her neck.

Beckett was about to lunge but he held up his other hand to ward him off, "One move Beckett and I'll snap her neck."

"You betrayed me." Beckett said, his voice a menacing growl.

"There's a war coming Beck, are you sure you're fighting for the right side?"

"Are you!" Beckett yelled. He saw Gannon's hand flex around Cara's neck, he had to get her away from him.

"I'm tired of living in the human world, having to hide and hunt them by night and feed off of them like dogs in an alley. My new Master has visions of a new world, a new existence for us Supernaturals, one of power. Where vampires will rule as the gods we were meant to be." Gannon shouted his tirade, his empty fist raised to the ceiling.

"Why did you come to me?" Beckett asked him.

"Because I was told to. My master sent his son to find me; he gave me the vile of serum and told me to find you. You people have no idea who you're dealing with!" Gannon shouted, becoming more agitated.

"Why didn't you just kill me when you found me then?" Beckett asked, they'd started circling each other, Gannon dragging Cara along with him.

"Because I needed you to lead me to her." Gannon nodded his head toward Cara, "She was supposed to lead us to the one my master really wants, but she's useless!" Gannon pulled a photograph out of his pocket and waved it in front of Cara's face, "Where is she!" he screamed at her.

Cara tried to focus on the girl in the picture but Gannon was frantic with rage now, his hand tightened around her neck cutting off her air. Beckett saw Cara gasping for breath, her hands clawing at Gannon's around her throat.

"Let her go Gannon!" Beckett ordered him, his tone dangerous.

"You don't control me Beckett, if I hadn't needed you to lead me to her, then you'd have been dead already."

"You could try." Beckett threatened.

"Now, I'll make you watch her die."

Just as Cara was about to lose consciousness she saw a flash of red. Spike burst through the window and landed on Gannon's back. Cara landed hard on the floor, she rolled out of the way just in time to avoid having Gannon and Spike land on top of her. Dragging air into her aching lungs, Cara watched the photograph Gannon had been holding fly out of his hand and land on the floor a few feet away.

Beckett pulled Cara out of the way as Spike and Gannon fought on the floor. Gannon had Spike pinned up against the wall and was about to sink his teeth into his neck when Oliver dashed in through the doorway. Seeing his brother pinned he punched Gannon so hard in the face that the force sent him flying back cross the room and tumbling outside the broken window. But by the time they'd jumped out the window after him, Gannon was gone.

Caleb and Feya rushed in the room, "What happened?" Feya asked, her frightened eyes surveying the damaged room.

Spike and Oliver leapt back in through the window, "Where is he? Cara can you see which way he went?"

Cara shook her head from where she sat cradled in Beckett's arms on the cold stone floor, "Can't – sense – he has – serum – " Cara tried to explain between ragged breaths. She remembered the picture and wiggling out of Beckett's grasp she crawled across the floor to where it had fallen and picked it up.

Everyone was talking excitedly over one another, trying to figure out what had happened.

"I knew that leech was no good the minute I saw him." Spike said.

"Was he working for Loke?" Feya inquired.

"What's this serum she's talking about?" Caleb wanted to know.

When Cara smoothed out the crumbled photograph and saw the young girl smiling up at her, she gasped.

Beckett went to her, and placed an arm around her shaking shoulders. "Who is it? Do you recognize her?"

The same eyes, so blue, the same nose, the same mouth, it had to be her. A tear slid down Cara's cheek and dropped onto the wrinkled picture, she looked up and met everyone's enquiring eyes, "Alexia."